SECRET AGENT "X"

THE MAN OF A THOUSAND FACES

AIRSHIP 27 PRODUCTIONS

SECRET AGENT "X"- VOLUME FIVE
An Airship 27 Production

"Dead Men Don't Lie" © 2015 J. Walt Layne
"Face to Face with Agent Loki!" © 2015 Andy Fix
"Devil in the Deep Blue Sea" © 2015 Fred Adams Jr.
"The Death Duel of Madam Rogue" © 2015 Frank Schildiner

Managing Editor: Ron Fortier
Associate Editor: Gordon Dymowski
Cover illustrations © 2015 Rob Davis & Ingrid Hardy
Interior illustrations © copyright 2015 Rob Davis
Production and design by Rob Davis
Marketing and Promotions Manager: Michael Vance

Published by Airship 27 Productions
airship27hangar.com

ISBN-13: 978-0692579244 (Airship 27)
ISBN-10: 0692579249

Printed in the United States of America

10 9 8 7 6 5 4 3 2 1

SECRET AGENT "X" ANTHOLOGY
Volume Five

TABLE OF CONTENTS

SECRET AGENT "X"

Dead Men Don't Lie

by J. Walt Layne

X had watched the pair meet in the café for a meal or a cup of coffee thrice weekly for over a month. They had no idea they were being observed. He was impressed with their subtlety.

Neither of them broke cover. He was always first. She was always a fashionable five or seven minutes behind. He generally took the liberty of ordering her coffee and roll. He generally ordered Eggs Benedict with an order of fresh sliced tomato.

Weekly one or the other brought a small token of affection. A flower, a love note, or some such. Always small, in perfect taste, and regular as clockwork. It wasn't enough to draw the attention of other patrons in the diner or raise the waitress's eyebrow, but X knew it was some sort of signal. At first X thought the dog had brought him a red herring, but then he picked up on the pattern of their rhythm. Their newspaper was the key.

That particular morning the man had arrived at 8:30 am, sharp. The Dutch waitress Imogene brought his coffee and they went through the ritual courtship of ordering. As the waitress whirled away, the woman entered at precisely 8:36.

The man had positioned a daisy at her place and she laid the morning paper on the end of the table. They exchanged familiarities in their way, but X observed that for their behavior and aphorism their body language was stiff and stilted. They never touched as you would expect intimate people to do. Their eyes belied their business, but made the ruse believable to the casual people watcher.

That morning she was upset. Granted she maintained her cover. He picked up on it immediately and was out of his element. It gave them both away.

His coarseness eventually got the better of him. He lashed out and she started to cry. "A man followed me around most of yesterday. Another was watching the house when I left this morning." She said it quickly, but not so quietly. This piqued X's curiosity.

The man glanced around, embarrassed. He started to put a hand on her arm and then stopped. He reached for his wallet and laid a sawbuck on the table, flat as opposed to the usual standing curl.

"I have a meeting. Enjoy your breakfast." He stood up quickly, crowding past Imogene as she delivered their order. He was nearly out the door when he returned, "Do you mind if I take your paper?" She tried to smile and handed him the curiously thick for a Wednesday, Daily Herald.

X already knew the paper would be left on the step of Dane Kerry an orthodontic surgeon. Kerry's connection remained, at this point, unknown. The offices were under surveillance by the Hobard Agency.

X laid his money on the table and followed the woman when she left the diner. He realized almost immediately that she was being followed by no less than three other operatives. The first was as obvious as could be. A very young man X took for a newly minted military intelligence officer based on his grooming and the fact that his walk was more of a march.

When the lady entered a boutique X crossed 42nd Street and from the six story scaffold on the front of the New York Mutual Casualty Company's new office building he watched and waited for the woman to reappear whilst the young op on the ground fuddled his way through trying to appear nonchalant.

The woman surged from the service entrance of the shop. X watched her across the lot toward the gate. He started to climb down from his perch, but stopped. When the woman emerged from the lot and started toward Grand Central Terminal a gentleman slipped from beneath an awning and crossed the street, following a dozen yards behind the woman.

The fellow carried an umbrella, but wore no coat. His henna colored houndstooth suit a color and pattern X himself had worn because of its particularly forgettable commonplace appearance, especially in changing light. The man's footwear was inconsistent with his dress, and X surmised that the sturdy shoes were more akin to a man accustomed to heavy work than suits and boots.

X followed, paying as much attention to the cadence of his mark as her pursuer. The chap followed her for a couple of blocks and X began to suspect that she might be aware of both of them.

The woman came to a sudden halt and the man who followed her turned on his heel and came directly toward X. He crossed the heavy traffic unfazed by the horns, grinding gears and less than civil encouragement to get out of the way.

Though the man who wore the houndstooth suit was far superior at the game to the junior agent who had initially followed the woman, he was no match for X's wit. When his head swiveled to an oncoming truck X dissolved into a crowd of picketing transit employees.

X emerged from the far side of the crowd of picketers. He glanced over his shoulder but houndstooth was lost in a sea of striking labor. He turned his attention back to the woman.

She was not where she'd stopped only moments earlier. X scanned the opposite side of the street, but she was not to be seen. He quickened his pace, hurried to the corner intersection and crossed the street. The lesser foot traffic made his search easier, but just as fruitless.

X pursed his lips and wrung an invisible rope. He listened for the sound of a woman's shoes on the sidewalk but heard nothing. There in front of him not one hundred feet ahead another man leaned against the corner of an office building looking intently at something down the cross street. The man was nervous, evidenced by the perspiration sheen only become obvious as X drew closer.

He started to pass the watcher, giving him a wide berth. That is until he realized the man was watching the woman and the heavy encroaching on her from an alleyway. X snapped into action, "It's not polite to ogle," were the last words the fellow heard before the lights went out. A short snappy rabbit punch and X rounded the corner of the building while the fellow slid down the corner of the building to crumple into a pile.

X covered the distance quickly and quietly, still deciding on his play. He and the attacker would intersect the woman's position at the same time.

Time slowed for him as it did in these situations. X felt the warm breeze on his face and moved through the viscous air with purpose.

The woman stood paralyzed with fear. X intercepted the attacker's knife hand as he thrust the knife for the woman's abdomen. X halted the blade before it plunged home, but his attempt to wrench the trench knife away was unsuccessful because of the weapon's heavy enclosed hilt.

The attacker turned his attention from the fear-frozen woman to her defender. He shifted his weight and attacked.

X parried the knife attack but took a solid left to his right cheek bone. No sooner had the punch found its mark and recoiled when the knife flashed in X's periphery.

The tip of the blade sung by with such speed that X didn't feel the shallow cut until a trickle of blood ran down the crease in his brow, alongside his nose and dripped onto his lower lip. Then it burned.

X recoiled, moving the woman back and giving himself breathing room. The thuggish fellow had undeniable skill with the blade. X surmised that he was likely a displaced or disgraced soldier from the way he lumbered into and out of the novice defensive stance.

X's light step to the left brought him inside the man's range of attack. He promptly blocked the knife hand and as he turned into it, seized the knife by the heavy brass grip. Hard blows rained on his back and shoulders, but X tore the trench knife from the man's grip, locking and breaking the wrist and elbow joints. The fellow barely uttered a sound, yet his face boiled red in anger and tears ran from his eyes.

That changed a moment later when the oaf backpedaled and drew a revolver. The fool raised it to look down the sight and X slammed a fist into the back of the hand which held the gun. He twisted the gun away with such violence a carpal in the man's hand was dislocated and the radius suffered a catastrophic break. The bone ripped through the skin, a ghastly injury. The scream was the sound of a wild animal wounded and cornered. X rendered him unconscious with a solid blow to the head with the knuckle on the pommel of the heavy knife.

He was off with the shocked woman before she or her attacker knew what had happened. X hurried her along for half a block before he stopped her, "Where are you going?"

She didn't answer and as he started to walk again, she just followed limply along. He knew she was in shock and he quietly cursed whoever had gotten her involved. X knew he had to get her off the street. He took the woman's arm and stepped into the quiet street. He had no sooner raised a hand and a cab U-turned from the opposite curb and pulled up. X nodded at the driver, one of Hobard's new men. The man's tongue tied and X went on alert, but the fellow's jaw unlocked and he gave the challenge, "Fine day, a bit dry for London."

"Old Nelson won't need his boat cloak." X stuffed the woman into the cab and nodded at the driver. "Take her to the Hobard agency. She's had a bit of a shock, you'll need to help her along. Tell Hobard that Mr. Pond sent you. Oh, and this is the woman that delivers the news."

The driver nodded, "Hobard, Pond, News." X watched the old taxi as it turned the corner toward 42nd street.

Looking back in the direction he'd come X wasn't surprised to see a gathering crowd. A number of police were already on the scene. One was holding up his club, looking around as if the culprit might hail him and take credit. While the gathering crowd harried the old officer creating chaos for the moment X hurried off in the opposite direction while attending to the cut in his eyebrow.

Making his way back in the direction of Grand Central X realized he was drawing a lot of attention and needed a disguise. He'd been gadding about as Elisha Pond, his oldest and most comfortable alias, but a business investor would have a very poor excuse for a freshly cut eyebrow.

Seeing his opportunity X entered the Glen and Sons Haberdashery to emerge moments later in the blazer and slacks of a working class newsman.

He'd no sooner slipped the PRESS card into his hat band and stepped out into the afternoon when a man in the street ran up to him.

"Say, you a reporter? There's been a murder." The gangly fellow said, his gravel voice scraping X's ear.

X, now in the guise of A. J. Martin, exploded in faux ambition, "What's that, pal? Murder you say? Where?"

The fellow pointed toward the place two blocks distant from which X had fled in a roundabout way minutes earlier. "There's a couple of flatfoots over there, or so says Mickey… You better get over there, once the detectives get there, they'll hush it all up." X shook the man's hand and headed off in the direction indicated.

When X arrived at the scene he found it in haunting repose to what he'd left. It started with a cap perched on a head, X recognized it as the place he'd recently left a rabbit punch.

Playing at his assumed identity, Associated Press reporter A. J. Martin, X fished in his satchel for a notebook and pencil, during which time he shoved an oxblood colored wallet into the inside pocket of his blazer. He also took a custom made Brownie Land Camera from the satchel and hung it around his neck. The camera appeared standard, but had an advanced internal lensing system and shot medium format images onto standard format film.

He took a dozen photographs of the victim and those who had gathered to watch the show. Trouble was the trench knife the man had tried to use on the woman and X, with which X had given him a stout rap on the head, now stood erect just left of the man's sternum. Someone had driven the knife in up to the hilt.

The wide crimson puddle suggested that the man had bled out. It was beginning to brown at the edge as the blood dried. X surmised that the blade hadn't stopped the fellow's ticker, but severed something large south of the pump such as the pulmonary artery or aorta.

X managed to get photos of the gathered crowd, and several of them with the man in the cap, whom he planned to speak with post haste in order to ascertain what, if anything the man knew about what took place in the intervening minutes.

He was waiting for an opportunity to follow the man away when NYPD's Inspector John Burks arrived on the scene with a pair of large and rather intimidating uniformed officers. Burks looked around the scene, but barely paid the corpse any attention. He scanned the faces in the gathered crowd and barked, "Who saw something? Does anyone want to step forward and help the police solve a crime?"

A few heads in the crowd shook from side to side and a third of the on-lookers started to disperse. The man in the cap didn't move. Neither did X.

Burks centered his attention on the scene while patrolmen started interviewing the spectators. The man in the cap started to pace as his opportunity to walk away seemed to be disappearing. X considered the same issue, but as a reporter he knew the fastest way to get out of there would be to get in close to the detective and become a nuisance with questions and camera.

But he couldn't question the man in the cap if he was in police custody. The man's nervous energy was enough to trip the suspicion of even the greenest flatfoot. X expected that Burks would notice if he hadn't already.

X raised the camera and obnoxiously shot a photo of the man in the cap, which did not go unnoticed. One of Burks' men looked to his boss for direction, and Burks left the side of the victim for a brief conference.

During their consultation Burks and, in turn, his pair of brawny cops took a long look at the man in the cap. Then Burks himself pointed at X and summoned him. "Press? You're a reporter, Hunh? What agency?" The gumshoe demanded.

"A. J. Martin, I'm with the A.P." X said, reaching for his credentials. The trio paid scarce attention to him. Their interest was in the crowd. X hadn't seen it coming, but this was what was known as a lateral pass.

"You got more film?" One of the officers asked, not looking at him, but past him toward someone in the crowd.

X nodded vigorously, "Yes, I need to change the roll. Just takes a minute."

Burks nodded, and drew X in closer. "Get pictures of the looky-lous. Odds are one of them is the murderer. Shoot the whole roll and get it to me at headquarters as soon as you can."

X wasn't as surprised that they'd bought his cover as he was that the detective didn't want the film directly afterward. He recognized this as not one but two traps; a chance to monitor his movement and for a surprise interview at police headquarters. He was not about to fall for either.

The man in the cap was also a person of interest. No one had come out and said so, but of all the people on the street, he was the likely suspect. He was the right age (old enough to be a drafted soldier just carrying out orders). He was neither forgettable, nor flamboyant and the way he moved suggested considerable strength for his size.

The fellow bristled every time the shutter snapped. At first his avoidance of the lens was very subtle. As X shot the crowd from various angles, that avoidance was apparent and deliberate to anyone paying attention. It was obvious that he didn't want to be there any longer.

"You got a problem, Bub?" An older officer asked.

The fellow played it cool, but not as cool as he thought, "Not a problem, but I need to get back."

"Back where?" One of Burk's men asked, taking an interest.

The fellow straightened his cap and didn't bat an eye, "I'm the dock clerk at Merton Textile."

"Merton's? You're a bit out of your way aren't you?" The big cop asked.

"I take my break at Shirley's Diner," he said adamantly.

X recognized the man's lie immediately and though he hadn't seen the man in the diner, he was confident that he, the murderer and the newspaper couple were all in some way connected. How he did not yet know.

"All right, let him go." Burks ordered, then turned to X, "Martin was it? You finished takin' those pictures?"

X nodded and started to unlatch the crank on the camera. He started to roll the film and Burks' attention was drawn away by a horse patrolman who he seemed to know very well. X never mentioned the earlier conversation; he simply rolled the film and followed the man in the cap away from the scene.

X developed both rolls of film and carefully selected the photographs he planned to deliver. He separated out the photos of the man in the cap.

He'd followed the fellow to Merton Textile in the garment district and sure enough he ran the shipping and receiving dock at the small contract uniform concern. At 4:30 pm the fellow left Merton's and walked to Mrs. Henson's rooming house where he visited a very old man before going three blocks south to an apartment. The apartment was in a dingy building off a service alley, called Lowell alley, after a cattle yard owner who was murdered there.

With the photographs sorted and the prepared collection loosely arranged, X bathed and put on the white shirt and blue dress uniform of his cover NYPD Commissioner Charlie Foster, an amicable but preoccupied public servant.

X had patterned Foster after a man named Duncan MacGhille, a nobody whose disgust for the status quo in his hometown's politic caused him to take action and eventually become Prefect of Aberdeen. As he aged the bureaucracy had taken its toll and as the man known as The Wolf grew long in the tooth he became that which he'd most despised. An old do-gooder destined to spend his aging days searching for the solution inside his own head. This guise had proven so useful to X that he felt almost at home in the character.

Betty Dale strafed her pencil across the top spring of her memo book. It was a pensive move calculated to alert the NYPD's Chief Inspector to her presence as he strode past her in the lobby of Police Headquarters. They exchanged loaded looks before he disappeared behind a frosted glass door. She tapped her pencil at the next unsuspecting flatfoot.

A door opened and closed across the lobby. A woman and her crying child exited the inner sanctum followed by Inspector John Burks.

Miss Dale couldn't hear what the woman said over the wailing of her child, but she distinctly heard Burks' delivery of the standard boilerplate, "Ma'am, I'm truly sorry for your loss. We're doing all we can. Don't worry, we'll get the men who did this." She fought the urge to roll her eyes, know-ing that Burks was halfheartedly repeating a rehearsed line which trans-lated to having no idea what to say.

Burks glanced around the lobby uncomfortably. Betty recognized that he was looking for an escape. Then two more women, obvious members of the grieving woman's family joined her as she got the company line from the Inspector. One of the women tried unsuccessfully to soothe the little girl.

Burks was repeating the nonspecifics of the case when Danny Perkins, entered the lobby and stood just behind Miss Dale. "Does he know about the press conference?" he asked quietly.

She smiled and shrugged her shoulders. "No, this sort of thing always goes better as a surprise. Betty missed something that was said as the la-dies walked away. Inspector Burks turned on his heel and nearly walked into Betty as the first of several flashbulbs exploded.

Burks held up a hand to shield his eyes, and Betty opened fire with a barrage of questions pertaining to the day's murder. She paused only as her heart fluttered as X passed by in the guise of Commissioner Foster.

The man in the cap sat at a corner table in Salvatore's, a tavern and supper club on the edge of Hell's Kitchen. The meal had been simple ethnic fare, home cooked, delicious and cheap. He was into the long end of his third glass of beer when a smallish blonde fellow approached his table, "Are you Mickey Shultz? The one they call Short Nix."

He pinched the brim of his cap slightly and glanced around the joint, "Don't call me that around here." He whispered as he stood and tipped his glass high. He laid a bill on the table and set the pilsner glass on it. "Vinnie!" He indicated the money he'd left on his way to the door.

The smaller fellow had been respectfully silent, but his impatience was not unnoticed. Shultz shot him a look. He was not intimidated.

On the street the smaller man tried to assert himself, "Mr. Shultz, your benefactor has..." Shultz gave him a sharp elbow and glowered over him, "Look here, I don't want to hear it. You people, whoever you are, got my brother-in-law on the hook for something he was into, no skin off my butt. My sister loves the guy, but she's not so wise. I love my sister and I'm going to be honest with you, anything happens to her and I'm coming for Levesque, Bennett, and even you Mr. Peck."

The little fellow let the threat pass and momentarily they walked on. "I don't think you fully understand the scope of our problem."

"Our problem?" Shultz asked, uncomfortable with the notion that he and Mr. Peck somehow shared something other than a square of sidewalk.

"Your sister does love her husband. She borrowed from a mutual friend to cover his debts, but the man is intemperate when it comes to vice. Her debt is more than she can repay and now they both find themselves in a situation that is, shall we say, tenuous. My partner needed some work done. Your brother in law had no problem in sending his wife to do the job." Peck's lack of emotion made Shultz's skin crawl.

"Yeah, I get that you people found a way to get her over a barrel. What's all that have to do with me?"

"I believe you are aware of the situation. Or does your sister have another brother?" Peck's beady eyes glowed black in the darkness.

"You knew that mug was gonna be waiting for her. If I had to guess, I'd say you set her up. You act surprised that I took care of it. Why?" Shultz wrung his hands and adjusted his cuffs.

"Mr. Shultz I'm sure even you can appreciate that the forces at work here are larger than your domestic concern. Your sister has been carrying information that has been procured at great cost." Peck stopped short of saying exactly what that might be.

"I believe you are aware of the situation."

"I don't care. It doesn't concern me. You and your pasty Belgian friend can blow. If I see you or any of them around her this is going to get ugly. Your sneaky business is gonna be real hard to conduct with cops and G men at your dinner table."

"Don't threaten me Shultz. They've sent me to put you in line or out of commission." The words were still leaving Peck's mouth when the knuckle sandwich hit home and blood erupted from his lip.

"You want to threaten me! How's that line up?" Shultz roared, a second sledgehammer right was chambered and cocked.

Peck shook out his white handkerchief and raised it to the gash in his lip, "I'm afraid you'll not live to regret that. He barely raised the pistol he held close to his hip. The nickel finish glimmered in the dim light of the street lamp. But Shultz was nowhere to be seen.

Shultz fled into the night. His heart thundered in his chest as he skirted the garment district. The hair on the back of his neck stopped tingling ten minutes later when he walked into Grand Central Terminal.

The sounds of the terminal soothed his nerves. Somewhere ahead a baby was crying and beyond that the sounds of Jacques Beaumont's coronet and the trio that backed him.

Shultz spent an hour walking through the station before heading home. His instinct told him to find his sister and leave town, but somehow it felt wrong to run. For all his faults he wanted to help her and see it through.

The sounds of the city were strangely quiet as he neared Lowell Alley. Somewhere in the night a couple was arguing. Somewhere else a glass bottle broke. From yet another direction a single small caliber gunshot. But it was almost too quiet close by.

He closed the door of his apartment and switched on the light. Across the room a somewhat familiar man sat in the easy chair which had seen better days, "You keep strange company Mr. Shultz."

Dalton Gregory paced. He hated to be kept waiting. His mood was made worse by the news that their reliable courier had been compromised. He was on edge about the fate of his delicate position. He'd recently been approached about managing certain aspects of a particular client's busi-

ness, and now he'd been asked to do away with the man who'd brought
him in.

Time passed and eventually Gregory decided to leave. He got in the
car and pulled away from the curb. The stink of the steam rising from the
manhole covers caused him to sneeze. He drove onward and a few blocks
later the road dipped. In that low place the steam from the sewers col-
lected and hung low to the ground.

As the car emerged from the stinking steam Gregory saw something
lying in the road and he mashed the brake to the floor.

Gregory slid out of the car and walked to the dark heap which was
further shadowed by the shadow play of dim headlamps. He was standing over it when he realized it was a man, he seized the limp shoulder and
rolled the body over.

"Holy mother!" He gasped, staring into the ghastly purple face of the
garroted Mr. Peck. He stood up slowly and reached for his cigarette case,
"If you weren't dead, you'd be fired."

A. J. Martin milled around the scene of the previous night's murder of
Mr. Peck. He took several photographs and mostly listened to the cops.
He'd tried to get there before the police, but he discovered that for a piece
of real estate with such a notorious reputation, Lowell Alley didn't lack in
the presence of law enforcement, especially those of the large, ill tempered,
Scots-Irish variety.

When he'd first passed by it had looked like a car accident. Some ill-
tempered easy street type standing by his car while a couple of cops peeled
someone off his bumper, not an unreasonable explanation. But a second
look told another story.

He hung around the scene until the detective arrived and started taking down names. As X turned and started to scuttle away he was nearly
bowled over by Inspector Burks. "Excuse me," X said in such a hurry that
he nearly forgot his cover.

Burks looked him over and X shuffled off, excusing himself quickly, but
the inspector recognized him, "You…"

"Sir? Yes, I'm A. J. Martin, Associated Press." X said with vigor.

Burks nodded and looked at him with keen interest. A bit too keen for
X's liking, "Will you be visiting all the nefarious acts in our city or is this
just a matter of coincidence?"

"Goes with the job, I guess. I'm always after a story." X said, sinking back into the Martin cover.

"I guess. Just odd that I see you at crime scenes two days in a row. Not just any crimes, both of them murders. Both times you're skulking around like you're trying to belong there. If you weren't a reporter I'd think you were the hawk who swooped in, made the kill and flew off waiting to see who came to investigate." Burks scolded.

X knew he was just about to be dismissed with prejudice, "So because I'm a reporter I can't be that hawk?"

"No, reporters are bottom feeders. Don't let me see you around here when I'm done looking over the stiff," Burks brushed past him. X allowed himself to be swept aside, but asserted an attempt at the last word. "I was on my way somewhere else when I saw the stopped car. I knew it was a story when I saw the starched collar and the cop staring at the same pile on the bricks."

Burks whirled around and glared at him, his eyes narrowed, "I don't like it. You people are a bunch of vultures looking to make a meal on a corpse. Just because I can't see you doing anything wrong, doesn't mean you aren't up to something. Get out of here, but know that I am watching you." Burks raised an arm and pointed up the street.

X heeled it up the street to a waiting car. He and the driver exchanged the challenge and password. He sank into the backseat. The driver said, "Where to, pal?"

"You see that starched collar talking to the officer?" X asked.

"Yeah, that's Dalton Gregory. He's just a small timer. Runs a legitimate courier service, and fancies himself as a player. Thing is, the people he wants to play with, don't fancy him." The driver said over his shoulder.

"Wait until he goes and follow him." X directed.

Minutes later Gregory was cleared to leave and got into his car. Less than a minute later he drove away. A moment after that the driver pulled away from the curb, tailing Gregory at a comfortable distance. Like most people, Gregory returned home after his ordeal. X made note of the address of the tidy home in the College Park neighborhood of Park Avenue near 96th Street.

"Okay... Satisfied?" The driver asked.

"Yes, now please take me to the Hobard Detective Agency." X said, tucking the pad and pencil into his satchel.

Katherine Hull sat in an interview room in the offices of the Hobard Detective Agency. She looked as if she'd been awakened from a dead sleep in a strange place and was still confused by the new environment. She vaguely remembered leaving Shirley's Diner. She didn't remember a man with a knife that several people had questioned her about, neither did she remember how she'd arrived here.

Leslie Cole, assistant to Mr. Hobard entered the room with something very familiar to Katherine, the newspaper she'd exchanged with the gentleman at the diner the previous morning. Ms. Cole laid the paper on the table and sat down. "Good Morning Miss Hull, first let me apologize for our accommodations. We thought it best that you stay here, at least initially. Safer for you here than at home."

Katharine nodded but she didn't speak.

"There's a gentleman here who needs to speak to you. It's the man who sent you here. He needs information that you have pertaining to your employer." Leslie said, in a no nonsense tone.

Katharine nodded again.

Leslie rose from the chair and went to the door. She opened it and admitted X, who was once again using his Elisha Pond cover. He entered, "Thank you, Miss Cole." He walked to the table and set his satchel on the chair. "Good morning, Miss Hull. Have you had breakfast?" He said quietly, projecting a much more mature and kindly persona than he suspected she was used to.

She looked up at him, and shook her head. He raised his chin a little and his eyebrows a little more as if to ask her to repeat her unspoken words. He was about to repeat his question when she said in a small almost pathetic voice, "I doubt I am very hungry."

X let a slight but genuine smile break at the corners of his mouth, "Well, I haven't eaten anything and I am starved." He turned to Leslie who waited near the door. "Could I ask you to call whomever you call and tell them to bring two of their largest breakfasts over, tick tock."

Leslie nodded, "I'll go and get it. Anything else?"

"Tea?" X both stated and asked by raising an eyebrow at Katherine who said, "Yes... Please..." Leslie left, closing the door behind her.

Katherine wrung her hands and cradled her head with her elbows on the table. X took a pad and pencil from his satchel before placing it on the floor next to the chair and then sat down. Her nervous gaze and trembling hands caught his attention as he settled in. He watched her for a moment and decided to follow his gut. "First let's have a chat off the record. I am

Mr. Pond, Elisha if you so prefer. Mr. Hobard's agency is a useful tool in my line of work. I need to know everything you know about the information you've been trafficking. I need to know all you can tell me about your employer, and who he works for. I also need to know whatever you can tell me about the other man, your contact who brought you the daisy. Among the services Mr. Hobard's agency provides are specialty investigations and protective services. You will be cared for and protected in exchange for your cooperation."

"And thrown to the wolves if I don't." Katherine's sober retort slapped the table.

X observed the young woman for a moment before he responded, "Yes and no. We're not in business of sending the unequipped into harm's way deliberately, but the circumstances in which you find yourself dictate a handing off for the greater good. You see Hobard has a duty to me, and I to my benefactors to support the laws of the city and state of New York as well as the government of the United States in reporting activities of espionage."

"Espionage? You think I'm a spy?" Katherine gasped, trembling and wringing her hands. "I'm not a spy. All I do is check the newspaper boxes. If there's a paper, I take it to the diner to meet Phillip. If not, I know he'll be bringing it. Either way, I deliver either to the diner or to the drop off. I don't see anything. I don't know anything. I'm not a spy." Her eyes misted, but she did not cry.

X watched the woman's body language and made a mental note of the clarity of her speech, albeit emotional. And her unwavering eye contact. "Well then, you shouldn't have any problem answering my questions."

She shook her head vigorously, "None whatsoever."

He took up his pencil, "If at any time you refuse, or lie, or try to evade my questions, I will turn you over to the war department."

"War Department? Whatever for?" Katherine asked, this time her voice caught in a parched throat.

"As I'm sure you know, they execute spies." X let that sink in.

Just after two o'clock in the morning X arrived at the residence of Dalton Gregory. No surprise; the house was dark save for a very dim light between the draperies of one window. He surveyed the house for some time and concluded that there was no security and no dog.

He wasted no time in approaching the house. He gained access through the servant's entrance to find both the mudroom and kitchen dark as he had suspected. He tread carefully, but soon realized from the sounds of a scuffle somewhere within the house that his presence might be of the least concern.

Misled by the nearness of the sound X went to the service stairway off the kitchen hearing angry men's voices followed by fisticuffs. Quickly and somewhat quietly he ascended the stairs to the first landing which joined the main staircase leading up to the bedrooms and down to the parlor, the source of the dim light.

X listened, slinking down the stairs slowly until the arguing voices became clear. From his vantage point on the fifth step he watched as Dalton Gregory tried to explain how a routine courier drop had become a fiasco now connected to two murders. The other man wasn't overly large, but came off as very menacing. In the dim light offset by the flickering hearth the man's henna colored houndstooth suit speared to drip crimson. X listened until the conversation had apparently finished. The as yet unnamed man was backing off when the fool Gregory lashed out at him to assuage his blighted bravado.

The other man simply pivoted, stepped inside Gregory's attack and seized him by the throat. "Mr. Gregory, I am not the simple street trash with whom you so readily consort like some bordello harlot. Your company's services were engaged for the simple task of moving information and now there have been at least two murders, with a dozen prying eyes looking into it. Discretion Sir, learn what it means or I will be the least of your worries."

Gregory was not a small man and knew how to handle himself. X observed that in the other man's grip he was careful not to resist.

Tense moments passed while the man in the henna suit controlled the situation. "I want to warn you Mr. Gregory, don't do anything that will further compromise our trust in your ability to manage your people and our business. You have a lot to lose." He shoved Gregory to the floor and was gone.

Gregory gathered himself and started to get up when he realized that he was not alone. He didn't see the face, but the man's eyes seemed to glow in the low light.

"Dalton Gregory, you've run afoul of the law and your fellow miscreants. It is time for you to choose the route your future will take." X said, glowering over him.

Gregory scrambled to his feet and moved laterally, trying to put distance and large furniture between himself and this new tormentor. "Who are you? I don't want trouble." He moved toward the hearth where a small fire contributed little to the light but gave his bully more menace. He made a poor play for the loggerhead.

"Well, trouble you've got." X replied as if bored, trying to put the man at ease by suggesting the pedestrian nature of this particular brand of trouble.

"How do you know? What business is it of yours?" Gregory demanded, closing his hand around the loggerhead with quite a bit less stealth than he thought.

"The league of nations takes a very dim view of criminals who broker in state secrets, especially those of benevolent nations sold to malevolent actors." X delivered the company line.

Gregory regarded him and X observed his eyes and mannerisms for the tics and tells which would contradict his words when he said, "I don't know where you get your information. I am not involved in any such thing. I run a courier service. My people pick up and deliver. We rarely if ever know what is contained within. It is primarily a residential service. Though I do provide a confidential and discreet service for organizations who can afford it." He said in a hammed sales pitch meant to sell X and bolster his own confidence in the story.

"For these organizations who can afford your discreet and confidential service… What is the cost of murder?" He beseeched, and as the impugned man started to deny the charge X went on, "The way I see it Mr. Gregory, your firm is an unlawful entity. Indictable for the crime of espionage. Who's going to hang for it? You? One of your partners? Or will you and they opt to hang it on an ignorant girl strung along by Phillip Loeb; the lothario lapdog of your silent client? Perhaps if I hurry I can ask your friend in the houndstooth gabardine. I'm quite certain that he'd go the full measure to avoid the gallows for your indiscretion pertaining to matters of discretion."

Gregory sized him up as X sank into a chair. Gregory said cautiously, "If I tell you anything I'm a dead man. Granted I don't do a completely legitimate business. Who does? I took a job to drop one envelope, but now I'm on the hook because the drop went bad and the courier flew the coop with fifty thousand clams."

X glared at him and spoke with mocking disgust, "Far be it from me to ask why you have a man you don't trust walking the street with fifty thousand dollars in these economic times."

Gregory considered his words before his reply, "The associate in question was a newer guy. But he had been reliable. Not a hip wart, but available when needed. No matter when."

X's assault continued, "So you're either too trusting or too stupid to keep track of such a sum."

Gregory bristled and looked as if he might lash out with the poker, but X continued, "Did it occur to you that your man may have been planted? Sent to gain your trust until you forgot to consider him a threat."

Gregory leaned back against the hearth, befuddled. "You think I didn't consider that? Proof was impossible to find, the man flew the coop. I guess you're not here to tell me where to find him?"

X shook his head, "No, quite the opposite. I'm here to solicit information from you on the particulars of your courier service as it pertains to the parties who have sent their man to you this very night."

Gregory turned to the mantle to pour himself a drink from the decanter that sat there. He pulled the stopper from the crystal vessel and laid the heavy fob aside. The sound of clinking glass and pouring bourbon preceded his turning and raising a glass toward X as if to offer.

X raised a hand to decline when something in the air shifted. Before he could react a bullet erupted from Gregory's chest, shattering the decanter and spraying the wall with blood and bourbon.

X started after the receding footsteps and the slamming rear door, but caught Gregory on his way to the floor.

Shock had emptied his eyes and blood filled his lungs, evidenced by the red foam he coughed. "G-e-t... G-get..." He craned his head back in the direction of the old secretary desk in the corner. "Ledger."

"Get your ledger from the desk?" X asked in a coaching voice, trying to understand. Gregory gave a shallow nod and tried to speak, but choked on a clotted glob of bloody foam.

"Who is your client?" X asked as Gregory's eye fluttered and rolled back. "The client!" X demanded of the dying man.

"Spieldoch." Gurgled his dying breath as the red foam boiled from his mouth and nose.

X shook him and slapped his cheek to no avail. He rose from the dead man's side and rushed to the secretary. He opened the desk and shuffled through the three small drawers. Pens, a pencil, a bottle of ink and an assortment of cast tin buttons were all he found. He raised the blotter sending the letter opener to the rear, lifted the desktop and was about to lower it again when he saw the small keyhole.

After a second glance he lowered the desktop and grabbed the letter opener from the rear pencil rail where it had sought refuge from his searching efforts. After a moment's fiddling the lock gave with a metallic scrape.

The panel fell open to reveal a moderately sized compartment. Inside, a small frame Walther automatic lay upon two legal sized volumes. One bound in red fabric titled "Accounts" and the other bound in green fabric titled "Ledger."

Thumbing through the ledger revealed immaculate accounting. Whatever his below table tendencies might have been Dalton Gregory had no little amount of business acumen. The "Accounts" book was at face value was in a similar state of cleanliness. X closed the books and slipped the pair into his satchel. He stood and slung the strap over his shoulder. The last thing before leaving the house, X closed the front compartment of the secretary.

Just before dawn X returned to his rooms. He'd taken the long route across rooftops and fire escapes. He chose to eschew the part of town that took "the City that never sleeps" moniker seriously.

Key in hand, X was about to unlock the door when he noticed that the doorknob screw was out of alignment with the bolt casing as he'd left it. He returned the key to his pocket and slowly withdrew the gas gun from his satchel.

Ready, he placed a light hand on the door and quietly, almost silently opened it and slipped inside. He closed the door behind him and turned the bolt.

X entered the living room in a rush, gas gun at the ready to find his benefactor Harvey Bates sitting with his feet up, reading the morning edition of the Herald.

"Harvey?" X asked, slightly confused at the clash of his assumption with reality.

"If you're quite done putting on your brash dandy put that thing away and sit down." Bates droned from behind the paper.

X looked at the gas gun one last time and returned it to the satchel before setting it down and hanging his coat on the tree. "Breakfast? Tea? Bagel? Cigar?"

"Good God, Man!" Bates slapped the folded paper on his knee, "I'm not here for a bite and a round of cricket. This has gotten way out of hand. The

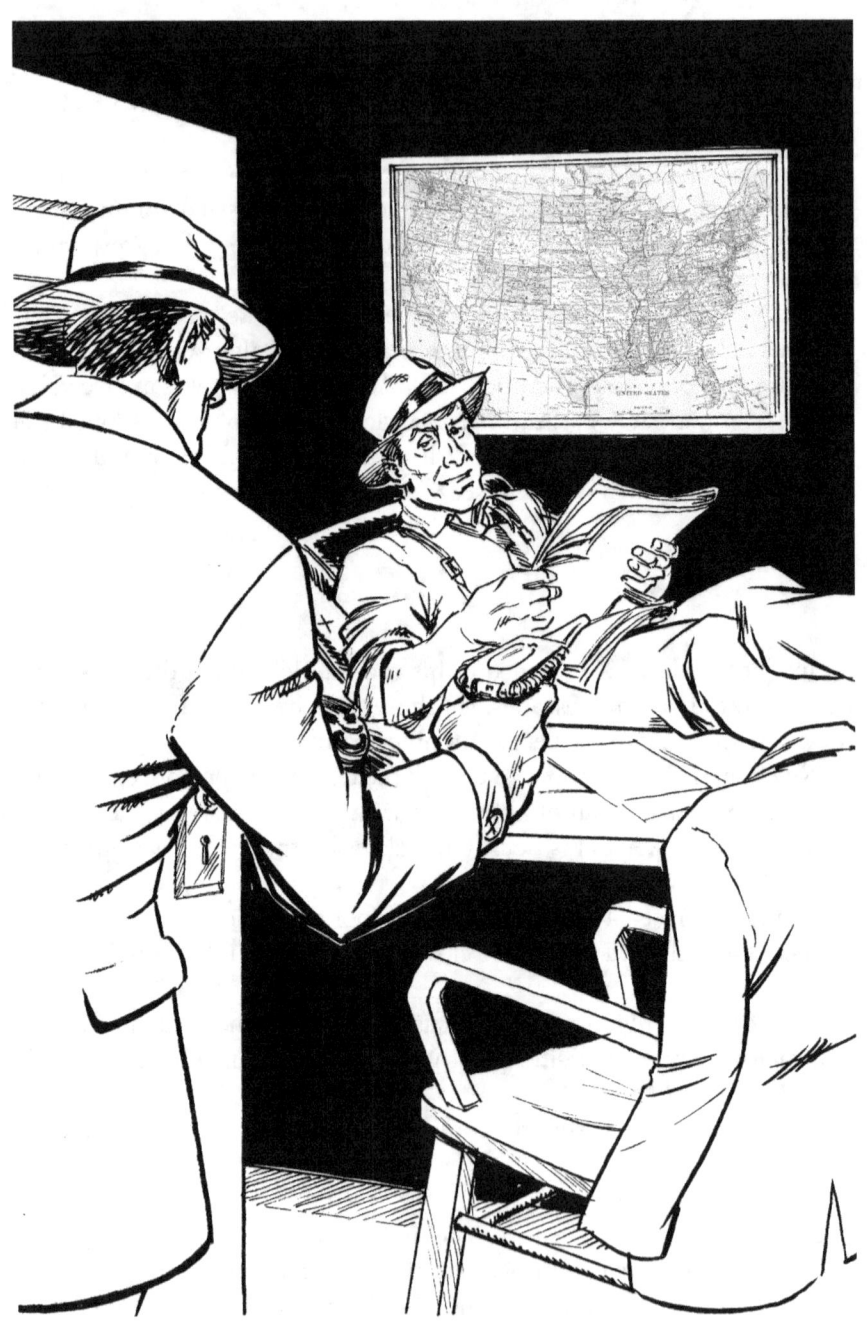

"...put that gun away and sit down."

foundation requested we look into the matter. They asked for you because they wanted a surgeon, not a butcher." Bates seethed.

X instantaneously sat up straighter, "Mr. Bates this is no street level thuggery. The owner of the courier service was tricked into this business."

"Still, three murders associated with this band of brigands is quite enough. Have you learned anything or were you planning to hunt the fox by burning the fields?"

X took stock of Bates and laid open the flap of the satchel. He withdrew the Ledger and Accounts books so quickly and thrust them at Bates with such ire that the man recoiled as if he'd been shot. "Have a look for yourself, old man."

Bates grasped for the books as they slid across his lap. He took up the Ledger and opened it to a place just a few pages in. Using four fingers he traced down the columns, glancing at the figures. He did so for some time and then laid the volume in his lap and reached for the Accounts book. His perusal of that volume also went on for some time. Someplace near the midpoint he marked the page with a finger and turned back several pages, for comparison.

"Did you see this?" Bates inquired.

X moved to the side of the chair to peer at one page and then the other as Bates indicated. "The legitimate entries have the company name and address." He turned the page Bates had marked with his ring finger. "Over here, the account name is simply a last name; Verne, Scott, Wells." He clarified again, moving from one section to another, fore and aft of marked page.

Bates gave him an encouraging nod.

"Has your man been through any of these files I've had Hobard's people sending over?" X asked.

Bates closed the Accounts book and the Ledger. "Well, yes." He paused in his characteristic way, thrumming his fingers on his chin. "Yes, and no. The information once decoded is only fleeting in its usefulness. We've not yet found the final piece of the puzzle."

X paced and thought for a full minute, speaking the details aloud. As he made a final about face he glared at Bates, "Verne, Scott, and Wells." He strode to a crate in the corner where a number of pasteboard tubes stood upright. He selected one and then another before laying a hand on a third. "Do tell, were any of these to do with shipping or supply channels of any sort? Perhaps troop movements, quartermaster, or transportation?"

Bates stood up quickly, "Why yes. How did you know that?"

X selected yet another tube and turned out its contents, a rolled and gum banded map. He took it to the work table and unrolled the map, securing the corners with several fist sized stones. "I don't suppose you have the files or remember the specifics?" X asked in the Schoolmaster's own tone.

Bates shot him a look of abject condescension on the way to his valise. He returned with a substantial brad bound volume stamped TOP SECRET and EYES ONLY with language limiting distribution to the US War Department and Office of Naval Intelligence.

Bates handed over the file and X opened it, tossing it flat onto the table sized map, covering the South Pacific. He switched on the overhead light and stared at the map for a long moment. "Verne, Scott, and Wells."

Bates nodded, looking smug behind his Socratic irony, "Yes, but there are no addresses associating the accounts. So for all they are those books and the three murders they represent mean nothing but a dead end."

Bates went on extolling the negatives, (a habit he'd taken on of late) while X shuffled the pages of the rather substantial file. His efforts bore no fruit until Bates' voice reached the grating tedium of a bastard file on an iron pike. He reached the end of his last just as Bates said, "Man, did you misunderstand? You are searching in vain."

X connected the dots as Bates words reverberated in the small room and tapped a finger on the file, "Not searching…found. Vanity would be unseemly." He placed a token on the map.

Bates was well into his post revelation dissertation on the fruitless nature of X's effort when his auditory nerve caught up and he dropped anchor midstream. "Found what, you say?"

"Verne," X said absently as he set a token near Newfoundland and another in Galway.

Bates started to speak. He counted the tokens, six in all before folding his arms and simply rubbing his chin thoughtfully. "New York Harbor, the James River, Port Galveston, Liverpool, Rotterdam, Galway. What's all this?"

"Verne, its shipping lanes. If this is true, then Scott is likely troop ship routes. And…" X said as he sought to verify the last token he placed.

"Wells…" Bates shook a fist and growled, "Wells is the whole bloody war. Operations, plans and scheduling. I have to notify the War Department at once." Bates sneered and swore a torrent of oaths.

X continued his work, saying, "We don't yet know what any of this is really for. If you put them on alert too soon and whoever is perpetuating this gets wind of it they'll dissipate before I can solve this puzzle."

Bates watched X's methodical search of the file, Accounts book and Ledger. He was impressed with the way the man dissolved into his work, not missing a beat even when he turned to take a legal pad and pen from the stationer's cupboard near the desk. His right hand making noted entries on the pad autonomous to the left hand skimming the file.

X listed the manifest number, vessel, hull number, port of origination, port of destination, and so forth. Nearly two hours passed before X spoke again and when he did it took Bates by surprise.

X shoved the legal pad at him and indicated on the pad and then the map. "Harvey, you must quietly alert Naval Intelligence on both sides of the Atlantic. I've discovered a hole in the dike that couldn't be plugged with the Titanic. As I suspected Verne is naval supply ships. Scott is troop movements and by volume they'll know something is up and have time to prepare. With Wells…let's just say they'll know what to prepare for."

Jean Michelle Levesque rose from his bed at just after nine that morning. He didn't bother being careful or considerate of the sharp featured young woman who wore only her long hair to cover her chest and a corner of the silken sheet over her backside.

He bathed and shaved, taking pains in his grooming and with his dress. He was careful to the point of obsession with the crisp white shirt, henna colored houndstooth suit, and the oxblood tie. He slipped his feet into a pair of highly polished leather soled shoes and wiped over their glossy surface with a wad of raw wool. He took in his appearance in front of the full length mirror and donned his hat and coat. Levesque grabbed the saddle hide bag and umbrella before leaving the suite and locking the door behind him.

He didn't speak to the elevator man, or the man at the desk. He simply held up the key fob as he passed and entered the Guest Postal Services office. He was alone, aside from the sound of some unseen clerk filling mail boxes from the rear. Casual and cool was his demeanor when he checked his mailbox. He hadn't expected to find it empty.

Every morning at this time he checked the box and every morning there were precise instructions on how he was to navigate the responsibilities of the day. He remembered the instructions he'd been given at the outset, if on any given day you discover no itinerary, assume that you are compromised and redeem your voucher. Today he would do just that, take a private stateroom on the first bathtub headed across the Atlantic.

He went to the door on the far side of the room and shook out his key. He eyed the sign which read, Depository: Long Term Guests Only.

The key scraped in the lock, caught on some internal bolt and would not turn. He withdrew the key. His second effort was successful, but the bolt retracted with the sound of a shot.

He opened the door quietly and closed it just so. Levesque selected another key on the ring and went to the box marked 321. He slipped the key in the lock and it turned with merciful silence.

Box 321 slid out of its slot on oiled rails. Levesque set it on the low counter in the center of the room. He opened the bag and laid aside the top of the safe deposit box. Inside the box was an espionage man's dream. A variety of weapons, a lock pick kit disguised as a manicure set, three different corporate checking books, each associated with a different international bank, two six inch thick stacks of currency of various denominations, including the infamous over stamped Reichsmark bills. There were also no less than a dozen passports and other travelling credentials from the various southern and eastern European principalities from where a man of Levesque's complexion could believably hail. All of it worthless by comparison to the stack of brown record jackets labeled variously as Verne, Scott, and Wells.

Levesque tucked the files into his bag along with a pill box filled with microfilm canisters. He attached a watch chain to his waistcoat button and opened the watch case to load the single shot firearm secreted inside. Lastly he placed two tiny glass ampules in his mouth, one between the cheek and gum on either side. One containing a lethal raw narcotic and the other an equally potent neurotoxin. Individually deadly, the combination rendering the most immediate assistance futile.

Levesque returned the top to the safe deposit box and slid it back into place. He secured his bag and rechecked the lock on Box 321. Satisfied, he departed the room and secured the door behind him, the lock again fired like a shot.

Jim Hobard carried a parcel tucked in the crook of his arm. A hasty conference with his client Elisha Pond concerning newspaper delivery had set a chain of events in motion that he didn't fully understand. He entered the Tarleton Hotel and approached the desk.

During his extended wait Hobard eyed the key board and the message box. Nothing stood out as being off. The place seemed to be on the up and up.

When the clerk returned to the desk he apologized for the wait, and Hobard played the part of confused courier. "Uh, yes sir. I'm s'pose to deliver this package to a fella 'stays here."

The befuddled clerk wanted to help in hopes the man wouldn't mention to anyone his extended wait. "What's the guest's name?" he opened the register.

"I forget his name, you'd know him... Particular sort. The kind of guy 'washes his hands after you shake." Hobard answered, hoping he hadn't given any clue that he didn't know the man's name.

The young man looked around and took a double take over his shoulder at the sound of rustling paper in the office. He passed a card across the counter and cleared his throat prompting Hobard to cover the card with a hand, then pocket it. The young man said loudly, "The Tarleton is not in the habit of discussing the affairs of its guests with outside parties."

"Sorry to trouble you." Hobard winked and walked away from the desk, falling in behind a bellboy pulling a luggage cart.

Hobard knocked on the door of room 321. He listened for a moment and gave the door the business for the second and then a third time. He turned the knob, but the door was locked. He raised his fist to knock again.

From inside he heard a woman's voice, "Yes? What won't keep long enough for me to put something on?" She was clearly irritated, and a moment later when she opened the door Hobard could see why. Her thin robe clung to her wet body and she was still trying to hold it closed and tuck a towel around her hair.

"Miss, are you here alone?" Hobard began with the cop routine, knowing that this part would go better if she had the wrong idea.

"Yes, when I woke up he was already out. Not unusual." She looked Hobard up and down. "Are you the police or something?" She asked, her French accent softening the syllables.

"Yeah, or something," Hobard cracked a smile and feigned relaxation.

"Did he tell you to come here? Michelle, do you work for him?" She asked, looking him up and down, fixing her gaze on his red hair.

Hobard almost tripped, "Michelle, err. Umm, yes... Hmm."

She smiled, and Hobard was struck dumb by her beauty just as her uncooperative towel spilled her hair to her shoulders and beyond.

"Come inside. I'll dress and make you some breakfast." She said with a seductive smile.

"Yeah, that'd be nice." Hobard said, removing his hat and letting her brush against him as he walked through the door.

She closed the door and tousled his hair on her way to the boudoir. "You can make yourself a drink if you like."

Hobard played along, not sure who was conning who, "That'd be nice, where's the bar?"

"Oh, there's no bar but Michelle keeps several bottles near the radio," she called from the bedroom.

Hobard poured himself three fingers worth of a bourbon he didn't plan to drink just for an excuse to look around the place. He concluded quickly that Michelle, whoever he was, didn't mix business and pleasure.

"Now, what would you like to eat?" She said softly in his ear.

Hobard turned quickly and sat her down in the nearest chair, startling her, "Oh! What are you doing? What is this about?"

"Miss… What's your name?" He asked as he sat down across from her.

"Janelle Rousseau." She said quickly.

"Janelle, I'm Mr. Hobard. I am, as you asked earlier, something of a policeman. I need your help." He began with the usual bit.

She swallowed hard. So hard that she choked. After a bout of coughing she recovered herself and asked, "Am I in some trouble?"

Hobard knew as the beautiful young woman wilted in front of him that she had no intention of being difficult. "I'm not sure at this point if you are in trouble or not, but your fellah, Michelle, if that's his name, he's in trouble."

She sat up straight and glanced around the small suite. She looked at Hobard and tried to give him her seductive smile, but it failed and she shrank, becoming no more than a scared girl. "His name is Jean Michelle Levesque and he is from a small village with no name outside Brussels. I don't know a lot about his business, but I will tell you everything."

"How long have the two of you been together?" Hobard asked, surprised that she folded so easily.

Her scared expression turned to molten iron, "We are not together. I am his property."

"Where is Michelle now?" Hobard asked, making a note to get back to the property topic as soon as he'd made book on client business.

"He is ordinarily coming in for lunch by now. If there is mail, he has to do business. He does not tell me this, I have followed him, and the mail clerk has followed him for me."

Hobard made notes, "Why did you follow him? How did this clerk come to be in your service?"

"Michelle is taken to being very meticulous and let slip something about a Rose. I thought he was seeing a woman. I was correct, but it wasn't this Rose. The mail clerk gave me money to buy food when Michelle didn't return for several days. I met him when he delivered a package to the room, much like you are doing today."

"So does Michelle know about you and the clerk?" Hobard asked, not playing hard to achieve genuine curiosity.

"Me and the mail clerk?" She squealed, trying to stifle laughter. "I prefer a man, a man's strength that you feel before you touch. Not the strength that is necessary to boast. If a man has the one, he doesn't need the other. Le clerk is like Michelle, intelligent, opportunistic, and very weak. If Michelle hadn't stolen me because my father owed him money, I wouldn't be with him."

Hobard gritted his teeth and made notes. He stood up and looked around. "Look, I ain't much and this is no proposition, but you deserve better than that. I know people who can help you get out of the city and set you up in a new life, away from all of this. Pack a bag, I'm getting you out of here."

X skulked about the White Star Lines facility at the port of New York. He'd convinced the harbor master to divulge the manifest of ships in port for a crate of scotch. The manager of the White Star Lines had given over the master passenger manifest for far less.

He'd no sooner emerged from the lavatory in his A. J. Martin getup when a disturbance outside drew his attention. As a reporter would, he hurried to the exit and to his horror as an operative; he emerged into a sea of no less than fifty Police Officers led by Inspector John Burks.

Burks stood on the bed of a truck, one of his men nearby directing the others. A number of reporters were gathering near the back of the truck. Betty Dale and her photographer were among them.

"Miss Dale?" Martin said as he approached.

She turned quickly, taking him in, recognizing the voice, but not quite placing the face. The photographer noticed and moved to intercept him. Betty's face lit with recognition and she offered her hand. "A. J. it is good to see you, even if it is work." She leaned close to his ear and whispered, "I didn't have time to call you, we just heard." She pecked his cheek.

"Heard what exactly?" He asked when Burks spoke up.

"Ladies and gentlemen of the press, thank you for coming out on this symbolic occasion. It is on days like today when we are able to defeat the efforts of organized crime. It was discovered today that one of the leading threats to the safety of our citizens, the narcotics trade, would be received by one of the notorious criminal organizations of The Five Points." Burks exhaled.

Flash bulbs exploded, blinding even in the overcast daylight. Martin was the only reporter who was not waiting eagerly with pad and pencil. Burks made eye contact and was struck with a familiarity he couldn't place.

Burks paused a moment too long and a reporter bellowed out a question, "Inspector does this have anything to do with the ongoing investigation of the criminal known as X?"

Burks wheeled on the man as if he'd fired a shot, "Sir, it is not the policy of the bureau of detectives to discuss open investigations." He broke off his colorful condemnation when the first of a dozen flatbed trucks loaded with crates stenciled Manchu Export Ltd pulled up a dozen yards away.

Burks slipped off the truck bed, hurried over and jumped up on the running board. Flash bulbs exploded, capturing the headline and banner photograph for the afternoon extra and the following day's front page exclusive.

The six door shuttle cab slowed to a crawl. The driver navigated the crowded drive at the White Star Lines building at the port. He waved to a couple of faces he recognized in the crowd. As he drove past the line of trucks, the two ladies on the seat behind him remarked on the number of police while the man in the back said nothing. A few minutes later he left the three at the gate for a ship, the RMS Rose of Gibraltar.

The ladies were the usual busy old biddies, but the man stood out to the driver, not because of his flamboyant appearance, but because of the saddle leather bag he carried and the way he handled it so carefully. As if it contained something very precious.

Levesque closed the door of the shuttle and carried his bag though the gate. He stood in line before the gangway and waited. As the line inched forward he slipped the ticket voucher from the inside pocket of his coat.

He caught the eye of a familiar face standing among the boarding crew.

A policeman stood to the side and a stately looking woman in a White Star Line uniform jacket spoke to him in a very nasal Yorkshire accent.

Levesque was perturbed by a very stout fellow behind him who was much closer than he liked. His every attempt to distance himself seemed to push him closer to either the policeman or the familiar fellow, both of whom he wanted to avoid.

He heard a car roll to a stop behind him, but he didn't look. A moment later he jumped when the car's engine backfired. Ahead a strong looking fellow called out, "Have your ticket and papers ready."

Levesque hadn't expected to show his papers and looked around uncomfortably. He fished in the bag and when he looked up, he was confronted by the ticket agent.

"Ticket please." The man asked and as he punched it the next man demanded his papers.

Levesque handed over his passport and reached for his watch, pulling it out by the chain. He opened it, cocking the tiny pistol within.

The man compared the passport and the ticket, giving him an agitated look. When the man alerted the police officer Levesque bolted. He depressed the watch knob, firing the .22 caliber bullet, striking the man in the throat.

"Jean Michelle Levesque," A. J. Martin called out as he tried to seize him, but Levesque struck him sharply and turned to run. But the man behind him, Jim Hobard slammed a big Irish fist into the Belgian spy's gut with such force that he spit out both ampules, and his breakfast. Hobard recoiled to avoid the vomit and the man slipped past him with Martin and the cop on his heels.

In Levesque's rash flight he ran into Inspector Burks who cinched him handily into a half nelson. "X, I presume?"

Though caught the young man whipped back the saddle leather bag and tried to strike Burks, "X is a myth."

A. J. Martin wrested the bag from his grip and opened the top, "Inspector, I'm certain that you'll find information here that needs to be turned over to the War Department."

"Officer, arrest this man," Burks thrust Levesque at the officer and turned back to Martin, but he was gone.

Levesque…turned to run.

X was taking a rare respite, a bite to eat with the comely Betty Dale. The venue for their evening interlude was Le Bistro an outdoor café with umbrella tables and a virtuoso violinist. Dinner had been pleasant, X had ordered for them both. A charcuterie appetizer, the entrée was an avant-garde take on tenderloin of beef with an herbed butter and delicately poached quail egg and a silk mousse dessert.

The waiter had no sooner brought the entrée and their conversation subsided when a well groomed Canadian Eskimo Dog walked up to the table as if he did so every day. The dog placed a sealed letter size envelope of the table beside X. The dog sat and waited patiently.

Betty eyed the dog with disdain, a look she shared with X when he lowered his knife and fork to inspect the envelope. She pursed her lips at the dog and returned to her meal.

X ran a finger under the wax seal of the Colonial Foundation and drew out the document within the envelope just enough to read it.

X,

Good Show netting Jean Michelle Levesque, but in a sea of spies he's merely bait for a much bigger fish. Get your creel and try the water at the Hunter Point Country Club. A black tie event tomorrow night was booked and paid for by Dalton Gregory and reserved in the name of J. M. Levesque. Our man Shapiro will pick you up at 8:00pm, he will bring you up to speed on the way. It's a couple's event, so bring someone to do legwork while you're indulging brandy and cigars.

Godspeed,
HB

"Miss Dale, how would you like to attend an event tomorrow night at my club?" X asked as he slipped the note back into the envelope.

She brightened from her wilting mood, "Why yes, that would be lovely. What time?"

"A driver will pick us up at eight sharp, so meet at my rooms; say seven-thirty." X said, reflecting on the happiness in her smile. The dog yipped just then, reminding them of his presence.

X put a hand on the dog's head and the beast shook his head until he removed it. "What is it fellow?"

The dog yipped again and titled his nose toward the remains of the charcuterie plate. X smiled, one dog to another, and slipped him a piece of Serrano ham and the last wedge of Picobello cheese. The dog chewed slowly as if savoring every morsel. When he finished, he took the envelope and was gone.

The following evening the car arrived at eight sharp and X opened the door for Miss Dale. The driver cast a shadowed eye at her from under his hat brim via the rearview mirror. She didn't notice, nor did she need to. X pulled the door closed and sat back against the seat, but didn't relax. The driver's eyes burned into him, but X pretended not to notice.

"The usual man have the night off?" X asked, as he slipped a hand into the through pocket of his coat.

"Must have. They only call me for specific jobs." The man's voice was thick, he wasn't accustomed to questions.

"How long will it take to get to Hunter Point?" X asked to appear unconcerned.

"Not long." The guy's eyes shifted off the rearview mirror to the congested roadway.

X slipped his hand out of the through pocket, slowly and deliberately withdrawing the gas gun and sliding it under his right thigh. The driver didn't notice, but Betty did. She shot him a look and started to fidget. X took her right hand with his left and from beneath the driver's field of vision gestured to her that something was off.

"Somethin' the matter?" the driver asked via the rearview. He wasn't trying very hard to disguise his irritation.

"Nothing. Just…" X said, matching the driver's annoyance in his tone.

Betty then understood and said, "What can I help if I have to go. A girl can't help what a girl can't help." She moved across the seat and sat close to X, feigning a spousal familiarity. "Why don't you tell him the good news, Eli?"

X was caught flat footed. So was the driver. "What's that?" The thick voice asked.

"We're expecting." She said, with a very proud and convincing smile.

"Expectin'…" The driver repeated.

X let him stew on that while he made over Betty the way a husband and expectant father would. The driver watched the road, but glanced at the couple a number of times in the mirror.

The car drove into the night. The driver was obviously experienced and had no problem navigating the traffic choked city. X was trying to plan his next move and Betty kept the ruse going. After crossing the Bronx River the driver pulled off the road and drove along the river bank to a dark spot beneath the main support and partially constructed deck of the new bridge.

"Driver, what are we doing here? This is not Hunter Point." X asked, feigning concern, knowing very well that they were less than half a mile from the country club and why they were there.

"Lookit, your shindig's cancelled. The boss takes a dim view of people meddlin' in his business." He growled.

"But… I'm going to have…" Betty started to cry, her tears only a partial fabrication. She was afraid.

The driver turned raising a pistol at the same moment X raised the gas gun. They covered each other, neither man speaking for a long moment. The driver believing he had the upper hand. X fearing only that if something should go awry what might happen to Betty.

"Looks like we got us a standoff, Mister." The driver said, cocking the pistol.

"It appears that we are over the same barrel." X started.

"Clam that up. You rich guys're all the same. You point a gun and you want to talk about it. Me, I pull the trigger and get home before the Fight Night Cavalcade hits air." The driver said, adjusting his aim. As tense seconds drew into minutes providence stepped in.

Providence in the guise of a horrendous sneeze. Something tickled Betty's nose and she was unable to stifle it. A very sudden and explosive wet sneeze erupted and she covered her mouth and nose. "Oh, ugh…"

X seized the opportunity. He patted his pockets for a handkerchief, affecting coming up empty, he looked directly at the driver turned gunman and asked, "D'you have a handkerchief?"

It was such a simple and human gesture, that the gunman lowered his revolver below the top of the seat and reached across his body to an inside pocket. He pulled out a white handkerchief and handed it over the seat.

X had turned slightly to attend to Betty and when the handkerchief came over the seat he extended his left hand, but didn't reach. The gunman saw the hand and took the bait. He over extended his reach and his chin.

Thrack!

X's back fist caught him square on the chin and the lights went out. His head snapped back in recoil and the gun clattered to the floorboard as he slumped against the back of the seat. Betty squealed in surprise at the sudden violence.

"Sorry," X said and handed her the handkerchief. "What say we get out of here?"

She nodded as she blew her nose. "I should have known something was up when you asked me to come out with you tonight."

He raised an eyebrow at her attempted humor and opened the door. He slid out of the backseat, gas gun in hand. Betty followed, but as she pushed off the seat, the gunman roused and grabbed her arm.

"Where'd ya think you're going?" He roared, scrambling for his pistol.

X heard her gasp and snapped into action. He crouched and raised the gas gun firing one round. The soda glass ampule shattered against the driver's chest and the two chemicals mixed, the cloud of sleeping gas was immediately effective and for the second time, the lights went out for the driver.

"We have fifteen minutes. We have to go now." X took Betty by the hand and pulled her out of the way as he slammed the car door. He half walked and half dragged the still befuddled Betty away from the car and along the gravel road track that led up to the main road. After a couple of dozen steps she snapped out of her daze and started walking at speed under her own power.

"What do we do now?" She asked as X fished in his pockets. "Where are we going?" She asked as he opened a pepsin gum tin.

She stopped and planted both feet, "You're having gum at a time like this?"

He gave her a slight smile and took something from the tin and pressed it into his right ear. He stood the hinged lid of the tin open and turned to the southwest.

Betty watched, wording her next protest when she heard a tiny burst of radio static and then X spoke, but not to her. "Hobard, its Pond. I've had a bit of a run in. My driver had in mind to put Miss Dale and myself out of commission for the long count. I'm on my way to Hunter Point. We're fine, but you need to get a man over here under the new bridge to collect the driver and his gun. If you have a man in the area we'd appreciate a ride home from the club."

A moment later he removed the plug from his ear and closed the tin. He tucked it away and started toward the main road but was confronted by the very put out Miss Dale.

"What do you think you are doing?" She demanded.

"I was calling the cavalry as you say." X said as he started walking.

"Cavalry? How about a cab? I want to go home, now." She said stamping her foot.

"Fair enough. Come along and I will call you a cab from the club, or have Hobard's man take you home. I will not leave you alone and I am going to Hunter Point. Someone went to the trouble of getting me out of the way, so I need to get there post haste." X said, asserting himself, aware of both her feelings and her feelings for him.

"Okay, but one of these days. You owe me a night out with no funny business." She gave him a skeptical look, and they heeled it into the night.

The Hunter Point Country Club wasn't exclusive to those wealthy enough to pay the extortive membership dues.

It was pricey enough to keep the low class riffraff out and level the playing field for big con grifters and diamond thieves. There were bored millionaires, high priced women of mystery, and men with secrets to sell. Most benign, some malign.

That night's event was a three hundred dollar a plate benefit for a recently purchased freshman senator. The fat cats planned to send him to Washington in style. There was a big band, lamb with mint sauce, a smoke filled bathroom for small deals, and a back room where a handful of nefarious big time players were about to sell out their country. These were not mobsters or racketeers from Hell's Kitchen.

On one side of the table there were the profiteers, butchers, bakers and candlestick makers who stood to pocket a lot of coin from fat government contracts and a chance to recoup their tax money and a hundred and fifty percent in ill-gotten gains for providing some wealthy fascists with the where and when for the who and what.

X's entrance with Miss Dale went mostly unnoticed. The band was playing a low tempo dance number and the room was preoccupied with choosing the proper fork. They found a quiet corner and sat down. A battalion of service staff deployed to their table and the sommelier poured the house wine Chateau Adirondack Syrah, the night's vintage a petite batch from 1899.

"My goodness," Betty said, over her wineglass to X who was scanning the room.

He watched the traffic of the service staff. Particularly those who emerged from the kitchen with small quantities not meant to be served en mass. The room was being served from service carts. When a trio of waiters carried trays toward an alcove beyond a massive stone hearth, X knew he'd cracked it.

"Miss Dale, how would you like a front page exclusive on an espionage ring right here in the city?" X said, drawing in the bouquet as he swirled the wine.

She stepped out of the moment and into work. "I have my pad and pencil ready, I even have a camera."

The band finished its number and the evening's master of ceremony said a few words in jest about the newly minted senator and then the man himself, Alan Spieldoch, took the stage glowing with the hubris of the bought. After a short list of self-deprecating back slappery he gave the short boilerplate about maintaining the status quo and locating ways to make more money before excusing himself.

X watched as the young man marched down the stairs, across the room and disappeared around a corner. As the fellow made the various turns to navigate traffic, he recognized the pivoted steps as facing movements. "What do you know about the senator?"

Betty lowered the wine glass, "There isn't a lot to know. He's barely out of college, grew up upstate someplace, studied abroad in the fatherland and his grandmother has a framed picture of him on her mantle wearing his Jungsturm uniform and jack boots."

X nodded. "There's a telephone on the greeter's desk. Call the police and tell them someone has assaulted senator Spieldoch and you're afraid for your life."

"Not a far stretch considering tonight's events." She said to X, but he'd already gone.

X quietly followed a young lady at length. As she exited the kitchen and made for the alcove on the far side of the dining room, she turned a corner and disappeared from view.

The alcove turned out to be little more than a landing at the top of a staircase with a small cloak room attached. X took the stairs quickly and the stairway led to a small open room with a short hallway leading off to the right. He walked toward the brightly lit hallway but pulled up short when he heard one man challenge another.

X moved quickly and quietly to the doorway and from the shadows peered down the hall. A man stood guard outside a heavy old fashioned timber door. Another man, who X recognized as the young senator Spieldoch stood before him and the two exchanged words, a handshake and the due guard and sign of the sacred lodge. After this exchange the tiler rested a hand on his sword and pulled open the heavy door. Once Spieldoch entered the tiler closed the door with thunderous rumble.

X watched until the tiler started to get bored and started to lean instead of standing ready. He walked very quickly down the hall to where the tiler stood and said in a commanding voice. "Good evening, brother. I was not aware lodge was in session tonight."

The tiler snapped out of his reverie and was caught tongue tied. "Well, it's not. Err… It is, but…"

X moved for the door, well aware that the tiler's duty was to protect the lodge and the brethren within. "I'll join them."

The tiler did assert himself, stepping between X and the door. "Look, you don't want to go in there."

"Why is that?" X demanded and he shoved the fellow aside and reached for the door. He heard the sword leaving the scabbard and it was clear that he'd underestimated the man's nerve. He turned and barely side stepped an overhand slash from the long narrow blade.

The tiler followed through clumsily and stumbled through a change in stance. He was not a swordsman. X tried to reason with him, "Sheath that sword and go have a drink. Do you know what's going on in that room?" The fellow thrust the blade at X but did not answer. X's response was to simply let the man's inexperience be his undoing. As he passed by off balance, X simply seized his sword arm, locked the joint and turned the man over on his head, dropping him in a heap. X drew his gas gun and pulled open the heavy door.

Inside three men sat at a round conference table examining several open file folders against several scattered documents. Spieldoch alone was standing, closing an attaché case. As the door swung open they were all caught by surprise.

"How'd you get in here?" the one X recognized as Phillip Loeb demanded.

"I might ask you the same thing Mr. Loeb, but you're here with Bennett, who takes his pets everywhere." A stern looking older man looked over his shoulder and then turned to keep an eye on X.

The last fellow was very familiar to X and momentarily he didn't want to believe it. "Dougie? What in the name of Bonnie Chuck are you doing here?"

Douglas Stewart, formerly of the British Intelligence Service avoided X's gaze, "Did you ever try to feed the kids on what honest work pays?"

X approached the table, covering the four with his gas gun, "Sit down son." He said to Spieldoch who simply glared at him. "Grandmum proud of you in your fascist pajamas? Will she celebrate you selling your country out lock, stock and barrel? How about when they hang you for treason, will she stand that photograph on her mantle?"

"You Loeb, just let Katie Hull hang for the both of you. Promise her the world after she gets you a job with Gregory's not knowing you'd steal Bennett's fifty large, just to get Gregory's people to run for him?" X growled his indictment.

"And you Dougie, no doubt you're here peddling the wares of a pig pro-vocateur, but you're op is officially rolled up. I wonder if the Black Watch will send a piper to your wake." X shamed his long lost colleague.

Senator Spieldoch listened to X's condemnation as it made its rounds and then buckled the flap on his attaché and picked it up. He made to leave but X intercepted him. "Where are you off to?"

"Despite your creative allegations, you have no proof that I am in any way involved. I'm a United States Senator and you are what? A busy body?" Spieldoch protested.

"I'm afraid he's a bit more than that." Stewart started to say.

"Quite!" Bennett stood up, turning on X, tenacious as only the aged can be. "You high minded schmuck. What'd it cost me for you to turn around and walk out that door? Fifty thousand? A hundred thousand?" He turned on Spieldoch, "Give him that case; I'd say a hundred and a half would do it."

Spieldoch tightened his grip on the bag, "The whole stack and a half? That's a lot of bread."

"That's enough bread to start a bakery." Hobard said as he shoved the still groggy tiler into the room at gunpoint. "Mr. Pond I'll take it from here. The police are upstairs searching the bar for evidence."

THE END

UNCOVERING AGENT X

Dead Men Don't Lie was my first Secret Agent X tale, and coincidentally the first of this character that I'd read. For this story I read a number of the old stories from the golden age and some of the newer tales. I wanted to tell a classic, elegant, golden age espionage story, but I wanted it to have the sleek feel of a modern spy thriller. I hope I've succeeded and I hope that you enjoy reading it as much as I enjoyed writing it.

There is just something that appeals to me about the innocence of the Pre-World War II time period. Our nation was still young and full of youthful optimism. In some ways the stakes were higher because the wars were more costly in terms of loss of life. People generally still loved this country and believed in Duty, Honor and Courage. I hope we get back there someday.

J. WALT LAYNE - lives in Springfield, Ohio. He is a veteran of the U.S. Army, a married father of three and a voracious reader. A prolific writer, he is the author of *Frank Testimony* a legal thriller set in Bedford, Mississippi in the 1950s. His short stories appear in a number of anthologies for Airship 27 and others. He is also the author and creator of *The Champion City* Series of pulp detective stories to be published exclusively by Pro Se Press (August 2013). He has written a laundry list of articles for *Backwoodsman Magazine* and is the former Op-Ed columnist for *The Albany Journal* (Albany, Georgia). You can catch up with him on Facebook as Author J Walt Layne.

SECRET AGENT "X"

Face to Face
with
Agent Loki

by Andy Fix

Secret Agent X worked the special putty with skilled hands, carefully recreating the face piece by piece. He glanced occasionally at the photographs pinned to the wall, refining details here and there as needed. The putty, a secret chemical formula of his own creation, was a perfect imitation of human flesh, and could be easily worked to mimic any face that Agent X had seen.

A flashing red light bulb drew his attention towards his radio station, and he picked up his radio receiver. "Agent X, here," he said into the microphone. "Go ahead, K-9."

"Status report on Operation: Loki, Agent X," came the reply.

"I'm putting together the finishing touches for the first phase of the operation as we speak. If all goes according to plan, we'll have the target in custody tonight and be ready to initiate phase two."

"Good work, X," said K-9. "But I want to express again my concern over this plan of yours. This foreign operative, Agent Loki, is a very dangerous adversary. His resources, intelligence network, and even his ability to disguise himself are almost equal to your own. And Loki has always eluded our efforts to capture him in the past."

"Which is exactly why I need to draw him out," said Secret Agent X. "My intelligence indicates Loki is in the States, so this may be our best chance to nab him. I know my plan is risky, K-9, but we need to change the game if we want to gain an advantage over Loki. We need to trick the trickster."

"And you're sure your current operation will draw Loki out into the open?"

"Yes, sir, I am. My operatives have been watching tonight's target for the past several days. He's French, not German, but he is definitely one of Loki's top agents. The target always works in advance of Loki himself, laying the groundwork for whatever operation Loki is running. His presence here in the city can only indicate that Agent Loki isn't far behind!"

"But I fear you may be pushing too far, Agent X. This plan of yours is uncharted territory for you, and if anything goes wrong, you and the entire operation could be compromised."

"I understand your concerns, sir," replied Agent X. "But I have good people working for me, and they'll know what to do. They're all quick thinkers, and they will be able to take the unexpected in stride. We'll get Loki!"

Secret Agent X glanced at the clock on the corner of the radio unit. "Sorry to have to cut this short, sir, but I'm on a tight schedule. I have an important phone call I need to make before I leave."

"Very well, X. Good luck."

Agent X reached for the switch. "Agent X, signing off."

The door swung open to a spacious suite. Without turning around, the man seated in front of the well-lit mirror said, "*Herr* Renard, please sit down. I will be finished here momentarily."

Renard took off his dripping overcoat and hung it on the coat hook. "My apologies for the water, *monsieur*, we ran into a storm coming up here." He sat himself in one of the armchairs in the room and pulled a cigarette case out of his white suit coat.

"*Achtung, mein freund,*" said the other man as he stood up and moved to the chair across from Renard. "That would not be wise, considering our current accommodations."

"Of…of course, *monsieur*," Renard replied as he fumbled the cigarette case back into his suit pocket. "I wasn't thinking…" Renard glanced at the man in the chair across from him before quickly looking away.

"Do not be ashamed to look, *Herr* Renard. As gruesome as you may think my scar, I wear it proudly."

"Of course, *Monsieur* Loki." Renard made an effort to look the man in the eye. The scar that ran down the side of the man's right cheekbone and jaw disfigured what otherwise would have been a handsome face. The scarred cheek twitched slightly as Loki poured himself a drink from the bottle on the table between them.

"Report, *Herr* Renard. What is the status of your preparations?" asked Agent Loki as he sipped his drink. He didn't offer one to Renard.

"I have identified several operatives of our main target's network." Renard regained his composure. "I am confident that we can keep them neutralized after the target has been taken out of the picture."

"Very good work, *Herr* Renard. And what of our objective? Have you gained any more insight as to how we may obtain that? We cannot continue on to the next phase of our plan until that is in our possession." He put down his glass and stood up from his chair.

Renard stood up quickly, as well. "Yes, we should be moving on that soon, *monsieur*. In fact, I am making the final acquisition later this evening."

The scarred German moved over to the wood paneled wall across the room and reached for a button on the wall. As he pressed the button, the lights in the room lights dimmed and the wooden panels slid down to reveal a floor-to-ceiling, outward-slanting window that ran the length of the room. The window offered a panoramic view of the thunderstorm raging in the clouds below. Peals of thunder could now be heard over the constant background thrum of the engines.

"Secret Agent X is a dangerous adversary, *Herr* Renard. He and his minions are not to be taken lightly. My entire plan hinges upon this phase of the operation."

He turned from the window to look back at Renard, and a flash of lightning starkly illuminated his scarred face. "Failure is not acceptable."

Secret Agent X reached for the dossier laying on the passenger seat of his custom sedan. He glanced from the attached photo to the figure walking along the sidewalk, comparing the two. "*Monsieur* Renard, I presume." He picked out the three additional figures that were slinking through the shadows nearby. "And friends."

X waited until all was clear before he checked his disguise one last time in the mirror, then he exited the car. The storms that blew through earlier in the evening had left the ground soaking wet, and he skipped over the glistening puddles as he made his way towards a building a couple blocks away.

He walked around to the side of the rundown chemical factory, feeling along the wall in the dark for a specific brick. Upon finding it, he pressed first that brick and then three others in a specific succession. He heard a soft click, and then a section of the wall swung inward.

Agent X entered the darkened building quietly but quickly. The side entrance he had just come through wasn't the only secret this building held, and he was eager to find out exactly what Renard was after. Harvey Bates, one of Agent X's chief operatives, had warned X that Renard had been poking around into various holdings of one Elisha Pond, holdings which included this factory. As Elisha Pond was secretly one of Secret Agent X's alternate identities, X wondered at what exactly Renard knew. What was Renard after?

X heard voices up ahead and got into character, rumpling his overalls and slouching his back. He grabbed a mop and bucket from the nearby utility closet and wheeled it down the hall towards the room where the voices were coming from.

The few overhead lights that were turned on struggled to light the vast room, and large chemical processing vats cast long, deep shadows. The group of men in a pool of light in the center of the room heard Secret Agent X approaching before they could actually see him.

"Who's there?" called out one of the three burlier men. All three drew pistols from underneath their coats positioning themselves between Agent X and the man named Renard.

"It's just the janitor," replied Agent X, as he pushed his bucket into the light. "Though, I might ask you the same question."

"Ah, *Monsieur* Phillips, do you not remember me?" asked a smiling Renard. "I sincerely hope you haven't forgotten our arrangement."

Bob Phillips was one of Harvey Bates' agents assigned to keep an eye on this facility, and he had reported contact with Renard a couple weeks ago. Renard had claimed to be looking for unspecified information, and this meeting had been set up to find out what exactly he was looking for. Secret Agent X decided to attend the meeting disguised as Bob, as this level of intrigue was well above Bob's pay grade.

"Of course I remember who you are, Mr. Renard. I just wasn't expecting you to bring no goons with ya, is all."

"I'm afraid I'll need these gentlemen for dealing with you, *monsieur*. You see, I myself don't like to get involved with fisticuffs, so I have hirelings to handle the physical confrontations for me."

Secret Agent X tensed, preparing for the inevitable upcoming action. "Physical confrontation? I'm just an old man looking to make an extra buck so I can finally retire from this crap job."

"Robert Phillips was indeed an old man, and he was certainly no match for my men when they dispatched him a few days ago. No, the man standing in front of me here tonight looking so identical to poor *Monsieur* Phillips can only be my true target: Secret Agent X himself! Ryan, we'd like him alive, if you can, but that is not absolutely necessary."

Ryan and the other two hadn't taken a single step towards him before Agent X exploded into action. In a blur, he pulled the headless mop handle out of the bucket and sent the bucket careening into Ryan's knees with a swift kick, knocking the goon to the ground. No longer a slouched old janitor, Agent X now wielded the handle as a Ju-Jitsu master would wield a bo staff.

The remaining two thugs started circling Agent X. One of the men feinted an attack, and while X was whirling to defend, the other suddenly lunged at his back. Agent X quickly disarmed the first attacker with a strike to the forearm that shattered the man's bone. The other man lunging at him from behind took a back-thrust from the staff to his solar plexus, dropping him instantly next to the first. X brought the staff around and struck the second man on the side of his face, dislocating his jaw.

Secret Agent X stepped over both men writhing in pain and pointed his staff at Renard. "*Monsieur* Renard, you are coming with me."

A click of a gun safety from behind him indicated that Ryan had decided to disregard the "alive" request. Without hesitating, Agent X fell into a roll and quickly disappeared in the shadows. Ryan fired blindly, sending bullets ricocheting off the steel vats and random electrical consoles. Sparks flew as indiscriminately as the bullets did.

"Ryan, you fool," screamed Renard as he dove to the floor. "Be careful with that thing!"

"Yes, Ryan, be careful what you shoot at," came Agent X's voice from the shadows. "Most things in here don't react well to bullets."

Ryan whirled towards the sound of the voice and fired off several more shots. Secret Agent X appeared from out of the shadows behind Ryan and clubbed him soundly on the back of the head with his staff. The thug slumped to the ground.

As he was turning his attention back to Renard, Agent X heard a door burst open and the footsteps of several more men running along the catwalks above the vats. This situation was deteriorating quickly.

Agent X produced a small pellet from one of his pockets and flung it to the ground. With a slight pop, the pellet burst and a cloud of billowing smoke quickly filled the area X was occupying. Several Thompson submachine guns chattered loudly, and the smoky air was instantly filled with whizzing bullets.

Secret Agent X ran between the vats towards the nearest exit. Though he was in little danger from being hit by a direct shot, an indirect ricochet could prove just as deadly. And even if one of the bullets didn't find him, one of them would inevitably find a sensitive piece of equipment or flammable chemical. Or both.

Almost as if on cue, X heard a loud pop as something ignited violently. Before he could dive for cover, a much larger explosion ripped through the factory. The air was crushed from his lungs as he was flung through the air, his head ringing from the assault on his eardrums. He slammed back to the ground, and a wave of heat rolled over him. His lungs burned for oxygen as he struggled to orient himself. The exit door, and the safety of the night air outside, had to be nearby! But before he could reach it, darkness overtook him.

Smoke and steam still billowed into the early morning sky as the firemen worked on the last remnants of the smoldering fire. When the Fire Chief saw Detective Burks already sifting through the ruined building, he hollered over to him.

"Hey Detective, you maybe shouldn't be rooting around in there just now. We haven't even finished up here yet!"

"Stuff it, Chief; this is a sensitive crime scene. I got a tip last night about this very building, and now we come to find it blown to smithereens. So, yeah, I think maybe I should be rooting around in here right now."

The Fire Chief threw up his arms is exasperation and turned his attention back to his men.

Calling to the uniformed officer standing just outside the gaping hole in the wall, Burks asked, "Sarge, how many casualties?"

"So far, we got four dead, two wounded, and, uh, some parts of others."

"Great, that should be a nightmare to sort out. Any IDs on the whole ones yet?"

"From what I can tell, most of these guys were crooks. I recognize a couple of them from patrol, ya know? Local muscle, leg-breakers, that sort of thing. One of the wounded guys claims to have been just passing by when the building blew. We found him pulling the other survivor out of the burning building when we got here. We'll sort his story out after he's cleared by the docs." The sergeant hesitated before continuing, "But, there is this one guy..."

Detective Burks looked up quickly. "Speak up, man, what about 'this one guy'?"

"Yeah, uh, let me show you. He's over here."

The officer led him over to where a wounded man was being loaded into an ambulance.

"Hey, hold up there for a minute, would ya? The detective here wants a look at this guy."

Looking down at the tattered overalls with the name "Bob" stitched on them, Burks surmised that there was indeed at least a worker on site when the explosion destroyed most of the plant.

"OK, so he's a plant employee. Poor sap was in the wrong place at the wrong time. What's so suspicious about him?"

"Well, that's just it, Detective, he couldn't have been in this place last night, he, uh..."

"Dammit, Sergeant, I don't have the patience to play guessing games! What are you getting at?"

"OK, it's like this. Some of my boys pulled a John Doe outta the river just day before last. Fish food, if you catch my drift. He's a dead ringer for this guy, even had the same uniform on. And, well, there's this..." The sergeant reached down to the man's face and flipped up a flap of skin.

Burks caught his breath. He reached down and grabbed the flap of skin and pulled it completely off. Beneath the layer of skin was the face of an entirely different man!

"Sergeant, lock down this entire block immediately and call for back up! No one gets in or out, do you hear me?"

"Lock it down, Detective? But..."

"Just do it, man," Burks shouted at the confused officer. "Don't you understand what this is?" He held the torn skin up to the sergeant's face. "This isn't skin, it's a mask! A very special mask, in fact. Only one man wears a mask like this. This isn't some poor janitor or even some local thug we have in custody, Sergeant." Burks paused and caught his breath as a smile slowly spread across his face.

"I finally have him. I've finally captured Secret Agent X!"

Betty Dale cut a striking figure as she pushed her way through the crowd of newsmen. Even as familiar as her fellow reporters were to seeing her there, many couldn't help themselves a quick glance at her curves as she passed by. The bright red dress she wore showed just enough of her shapely legs to make even the most honorable man's knees weak. Betty used this to her advantage as she forced her way through the crowd up to the front of the room.

As Betty neared the podium, one stout figure in a rumpled brown suit failed to give way.

"That's not very gentlemanly of you, Sam," said Betty as she playfully elbowed him in the ribs from behind.

"That's OK, Betty, I ain't accused of being a gentleman very often anyway," replied Sam, glancing over his shoulder at her. If he noticed the ashes that fell from his cigar onto his suit coat, he didn't bother to brush them off. "Yer just mad that I'm immune to yer feminine wiles. You know I prefer brunettes."

Betty ignored his quip, not wanting to give him any satisfaction. She flipped her long blonde hair out of her face as she pulled out her notepad and pencil

"So, what do you think this is all about, Sam? The Police Commissioner doesn't call a press conference unless it's something big. You think it has to do with the President being in town?"

"I don't think so, kiddo." Another glance back, another dash of ashes added to the collection on his lapel. "The President doesn't get here until this afternoon, and there's been a buzz of activity on the streets. There was a four-alarm fire last night, and the cops shut down that whole block just after dawn. Nah, this is something bigger, I betcha."

Betty put a hand on Sam's shoulder to steady herself as she stood on her tiptoes and looked back over the crowd of reporters. "Say, you haven't seen A.J. Martin come through here, have you Sam?"

"Nah, haven't seen him at all," answered Sam with another backward glance. Betty was sure that his suit coat would start smoldering if he kept that up. "In fact, that fresh-faced young kid over there is representing Associated Press today," he continued. "Seems the AP couldn't dig up Martin, either. What gives? You two are usually pallin' around together."

"I'm not sure, Sam," said Betty. The slight crinkle of her brow betrayed the worry she was starting to feel. Sam couldn't have known that A.J. Martin was really one of Secret Agent X's disguises. Only she was close enough to the secretive X to know that. She also knew that if something big and mysterious were going on in the city that Agent X was sure to be interested. His absence at the press conference was definitely unusual. "I'm sure he'll turn up," she added with a nervous smile.

Just then, the low murmur of conversation in the room died down. Betty turned back to the podium to see Commissioner Foster walking into the room accompanied by a smiling Detective Burks. Betty's slight pang of worry began to knit her brows together a little tighter. Detective Burks had an obsession with ending what he thought to be Secret Agent X's criminal career. Seeing him standing up there next to the Commissioner and wearing a self-satisfied grin on his face was not a good sign.

"Gentlemen—and lady—of the press," began the Commissioner with a slight nod to Betty, "We called this press conference today to announce an important arrest." The room grew quiet as the crowd of reporters held its collective breath. "On the eve of the President of the United States visiting our fair city, a team of crack detectives, led by Detective Burks here, uncovered a ring of criminals planning a major operation. The leader of this crime ring was a man that, until now, was thought to be little more than a rumor by most."

Betty could feel a bead of sweat trickling down her brow. Her mind raced for any possible explanation other than the one she feared most. It couldn't possibly be him!

"Detective Burks here has been hunting this man relentlessly, but he has always managed to elude capture," continued the Commissioner.

Betty's head was starting to swim. Secret Agent X was too careful, too skillful. They weren't talking about him!

"This man is known among the law enforcement community only by a code name." Commissioner Foster paused and looked around the silent room.

"He is known as Secret Agent X."

The room exploded around Betty with noise and motion as everyone started waving their arms and shouting questions all at once. Betty's vision blurred, and the floor and ceiling suddenly switched positions. She felt herself falling into darkness when a pair of strong arms wrapped around her shoulders.

"Hey, kiddo! You okay," came Sam's concerned voice.

Betty shook her head clear and blinked away tears. "I-I'm fine, Sam," said Betty as she steadied herself. "I think it's just the heat getting to me."

Betty heard the Commissioner announce, "I'll now turn things over to Detective Burks to answer any of your questions."

As she regained her composure, Betty saw Detective Burks point to a man in the corner.

"Simon Kirby, Timely News," said the man as introduction. "Detective, if this Agent X is such a mystery man, how do you know it's him you have in custody?"

"A good question, Mr. Kirby," answered Burks. "Last night, we received a tip that Secret Agent X would be active in our city. That tip lead us to a four-alarm fire in progress in an industrial block near downtown. I have been personally tracking Agent X for several years, and I have become familiar with the methods and tools he uses to perpetrate his crimes. These items are of such a nature that only Agent X would have access to them. A wounded man at the scene had several of these items in his possession. This strongly suggests that the man in question is Secret Agent X."

The mass of newsmen all started calling for Burks' attention again. The detective looked around the room for the next reporter he would answer.

"H-how is he," came a soft voice. Betty was surprised to realize that it was hers.

Detective Burks stood at the podium just a few feet away from Betty, but he couldn't possibly have made out what she said over the din the other reporters were making. Burks said, "I'm sorry, Miss Dale, I didn't hear your question."

Betty felt every eye in the room on her. Steeling her resolve, Betty stood up straight and said in a firm voice, "Betty Dale, from the Herald. You mentioned the prisoner was wounded. Is he being treated? Are his injuries life threatening?"

"The prisoner is at Memorial Hospital," replied Burks. "He is currently still unconscious, but he is in stable condition. The doctors tell me that he should survive, but it's unknown what the extent of the damage he may have suffered from the blast will be until he comes out of his coma."

Betty felt faint again upon hearing this, but she managed to maintain her balance this time. Secret Agent X was still alive, but at what price?

Betty Dale walked slowly through the hallways of Memorial hospital. As she rounded the corner, she saw a patient room with a lone police officer standing guard in front of the door. The stark hospital lighting didn't do her appearance any favors; her umbrella had protected her from the rain, but the stress of the day had very likely completely wrecked her makeup. But she put on her best smile, unbuttoned another button of her blouse, and sauntered over to the room.

"Mick? Mick Finnley, is that you," she asked as she approached the young police officer in front of the door.

Mick's eyes nearly bugged out of his head as they took in Betty's figure.

"Um... uh...," was the best he could manage in response.

Betty wrapped her arm through the officer's arm and reached up to give him a peck on the cheek. "How's your dad?"

"He's well, enough, ma'am, thank you," replied Mick. "Retirement isn't exciting enough for him, though. He misses the guys on the force, especially... um..."

"Especially my dad," finished Betty. "Yeah, I remember how close our families were." Betty's smile brightened. "It's so good to see you again!"

"...sorry, Miss Dale, I didn't hear your question."

"What, uh, what brings you around here, Betty," asked Mick as he nervously tried to untwine Betty's arm from his.

"Other than chatting with an old family friend? Oh, I guess I am here on business, now that you ask."

"Betty, there's no way I can let you in this room," said Mick, now prying Betty's arm off of his and actively pushing her away. "Detective Burks would have my badge!"

"Mick, I need just a few minutes," Betty pleaded. "I'll be in and out before anyone notices, I promise!"

"Oh gosh, Betty, I just..."

Betty didn't wait for Mick to even finish his thought. She reached up and pecked him on the other cheek, and then slid around him and opened the door. Before she disappeared into the room, she glanced back at him and said, "Thanks!"

Once in the dimly lit room, Betty gently laid her umbrella against the chair and approached the figure in the bed hesitantly. The man's shallow breathing was barely audible, but it was there. Tears welled up in her eyes as she gingerly ran her fingers down the side of his face. What wasn't covered by bandages was deformed by swollen bruises.

"Oh, what have they done to you," she whispered softly as the tears started streaming down her cheeks.

Just then, the door opened and the stark light from the hallway spilled in. Betty heard Mick whisper, "Miss Dale, please, you gotta go now. Detective Burks is on his way up."

Betty could hear the desperation in his voice.

"Of course, Mick," Betty replied. "I'll be right out."

Detective Burks strode quickly down the hospital hallway towards the room his prisoner was in. The two men behind him had to walk swiftly to keep pace with the detective. Burks' growing frustration with his inability to interrogate the man in the room showed through the scowl on his face. Even in a coma, Secret Agent X still found ways to vex Burks.

As they rounded the last corner before the room, Detective Burks stopped abruptly, just barely managing to avoid knocking the woman in front of him to the ground.

"Blast it, would you watch where... Oh, Miss Dale, I'm terribly sorry," said Burks, suddenly recognizing the woman he had nearly bowled over.

Looking suspiciously from her to the officer standing guard outside of Agent X's room, Burks continued, "May I ask what you are doing here?"

"I was trying to do my job," Betty answered, "but Officer Stoneface over there wouldn't even look at me, much less let me interview your prisoner."

"Miss Dale," said Burks, trying very hard to control his temper, "I must insist that you leave immediately. Unless you want to be charged with interfering with an ongoing police investigation?"

"But what bigger story is there than the capture of Secret Agent X?" argued Betty.

Detective Burks face darkened as his temper rose. "Miss Dale...," he began through tight lips. Just then, the civilian standing behind him stepped forward.

"Inspector Burks, won't you introduce me to the lovely young lady," said the man with a thick French accent.

Burks cringed when he saw Betty's eyes light up with interest. She could obviously see the soot covering the man's white suit and his left arm hanging in a sling. Add to the fact that he was in this hospital in front of this room with Burks, and any half-way competent reporter could make the connection between him and the Agent X case. And Betty Dale was a top tier reporter.

Betty extended her hand to the stranger and said, "Betty Dale, crime reporter for the Herald. And you are...?"

"*Bon jour, Mademoiselle*," responded the Frenchman. "Sebastian Renard, at your service." Renard took Betty's extended hand and pressed it to his lips. "Had I known such beauty could be found in this city, I would have left Paris a long time ago."

Betty smiled demurely in response to the handsome Frenchman's obvious flattery, but Burks could still see the spark in her eye. She was still after her story, and Renard must look like a tempting target now that she had failed to get to Agent X.

"Before you ask, Dale, the answer is no," interjected Burks before this conversation could go any further. "Mr. Renard is a material witness to an ongoing police investigation, and he will not be made available to the press at this time."

Before Betty could argue, Renard spoke up again. "Alas, *Mademoiselle*. Perhaps when Inspector Burks and I are done, I will come find you and we can fly away and get married and spend all the rest of our days together." With a broad wink and a smile that turned up the corners of his pencil-thin mustache, Renard kissed her hand once more. When the detective with him gave him a nudge in the direction of the room, Renard bowed with a flourish and allowed himself to be escorted away.

Betty frowned at Burks before she walked away down the hall towards the elevator. Burks made sure she actually got on the elevator and the door closed behind her before he turned towards the room.

"Officer Finnley," Burks said after glancing at the guard's badge. "No one has entered or left this room since you got here, correct?"

"Ms. Dale wanted to, sir," replied the obviously nervous young officer, "but I told her she couldn't."

"Very good, Finnley, as you were," said Burks.

"Thank you, sir."

Burks opened the door to enter the room when he paused and turned back to Finnley.

"Oh, and Finnley," he said.

"Yes, sir?"

"Wipe that lipstick off of your face."

Burks closed the door behind him. The light was on, but the man in the bed was as oblivious to that as he was to the men in his room.

"Mr. Renard, is this the man you saw last night," asked Burks.

Renard looked at the man's face before shrugging. "I don't know, Inspector. How can I tell who he is with all the bandages and the bruises? I can tell you that the man I pulled from that building was an old man, and this man here doesn't look nearly as old."

"Tell me again," said Burks, "what exactly was it you were doing in that area at that time of night?"

"As I mentioned earlier, Inspector," said Renard calmly, "I arrived just recently from Europe aboard the airship, the *Gotterdammerung*. Such travel is much faster than by sea, you see, so I have not yet adjusted to the new daylight schedule. I still wake up several hours before the sun comes up. It's all very inconvenient."

"I'm sure it is," replied Burks.

"And so, as the city around me lay sleeping," continued Renard, "I decided to go for a walk. I do so love the smell of the fresh air after a good rainstorm has washed it clean." Renard smiled innocently at the Detective.

"Mmm hmm," grunted Burks suspiciously. "And what brought you over here to America in such a luxurious fashion? A ticket aboard the *Gotterdammerung* ain't cheap."

"Why, I am a musician, Inspector. I play in the string quartet onboard the airship, where I am a master of the cello." Renard mimed pulling a bow over an invisible cello in front of him.

Burks glanced at the detective standing behind Renard, who simply shrugged in response. The detective pinched the bridge of his nose and sighed.

"Very well, Mr. Renard," said Burks. "You are free to go. Just make sure you don't leave town. I'm sure we'll be talking to you again soon."

Renard tapped his good hand to his brow and stepped past Detective Burks, grabbing the umbrella leaning against the chair as he left the room.

After another sigh, Burks looked again at the other detective. "We need to keep tabs on him," Burks said.

Persistence and patience, those were the two qualities that made for a good reporter. At least, that's what Betty always believed. Now was one of those times where those qualities paid dividends.

It was actually her umbrella that caught her attention. Somehow, Renard had it hanging from his arm when he walked by Betty in the hospital lobby. She smiled slyly to herself as Renard blissfully walked by her without even glancing her way. Like a lioness hunting her prey, Betty began stalking Renard, following closely, but not too close to be noticed.

Renard exited through the revolving door into the late afternoon outside. Betty hurried to follow, but a pair of ancient nuns entering the hospital slowed the door to a crawl. Betty bit her lip in frustration; the last thing she needed right now was to be cursing at nuns.

When she finally spilled out onto the sidewalk, Betty realized that she had lost Renard. Now she cursed freely, only at herself. She should really leave this cloak and dagger stuff to Secret Agent X. Steeling her resolve for what felt like the hundredth time that day, Betty looked both ways before deciding to head to the right.

Luck. Luck definitely needed to be added to her list of qualities a good reporter needs to have. As her luck would have it, she had chosen the right direction. After a couple blocks of walking, Betty caught a glimpse of a white suit disappearing into an alley about half a block ahead.

Betty hurried down the sidewalk, slowing as she neared the alley. The setting sun was hidden by the buildings now, so the alley was cloaked in darkness. Any meeting being held in a dark alley was a meeting the participants wanted to keep secret.

Betty could make out some quiet talking, so she leaned closer in an attempt to make out what was being said.

"... and you're certain it was him," asked one voice with a European accent of some sort. German?

"Of course, *monsieur*," replied Renard. "The armed guard in front of the room should be enough, but the visitor he had just before I arrived was all the confirmation I needed."

"And who was that," asked the first voice.

"Why, the lovely Betty Dale, *monsieur*. We know from our investigations that Ms. Dale is an operative of Secret Agent X. And I saw her with my own eyes, she was very distraught. As if she were visiting an ill friend more than as if she were a reporter tracking down a story."

"Excellent," responded the other. "Our plan is progressing nicely, *Herr* Renard. Agent X is out of the way, and now you have delivered the final component that I need. You may go. I have final preparations to make before tomorrow night's dinner party."

A moment later, Sebastian Renard approached the mouth of the alley and carefully looked both ways. Betty was pressed up tightly against the wall of the building, partially hidden by a downspout and the deep shadows cast by the setting sun. She was sure that Renard had seen her, but he exited the alley and continued on down the street, twirling her umbrella in his good hand, seemingly unaware of her presence.

Betty resisted the urge to follow him. First she wanted to see who it was Renard had been talking to. She took a step towards the alley to take a peek, but someone else was already coming out. She looked up at the man and swallowed a yelp. This was absolutely the last person in the world she was expecting to be exiting that alley.

"A.J. Maritn," she exclaimed, half surprised and half confused. "Wait...? How did...? Who... ?" She couldn't quite get her brain to form a complete sentence. She looked around as if someone nearby could explain everything to her.

A.J. Martin looked her up and down appraisingly before responding, "Hiya, toots! Fancy meeting you here."

It could have been the fading light, but something about Martin's face didn't look quite right. His smile was stiff and didn't quite reach his eyes, and his cheek twitched ever so slightly every now and then.

"A.J., I... What's going on? What are you doing here?"

"Cracking this story wide open, Betty! Come here and look what I have." Martin turned back towards the alley and gestured for her to follow him.

Hesitantly, Betty stepped towards the alley. A.J. Martin was just a cover identity for Secret Agent X, not a real reporter. So who was this guy using one of X's disguises? And where was the German man Renard had been talking to? Curiosity got the best of her. Ignoring the alarm bells going off in the back of her head, Betty followed A.J. Martin into the darkness of the alley.

She hadn't taken three steps into the alley before she regretted that decision. As she followed Martin, she noticed two forms step from the shadows on either side of her to block her way back to the sidewalk. She turned back towards Martin and nearly ran into him.

A.J. Martin stood stock still with his hands held behind his back glowering down at Betty. "It is unfortunate that you happened to be here tonight, *Fraulein* Dale," he said in a voice that was most certainly not American. "You are quite the lovely creature, but we cannot have you revealing to anyone the discussion you just overheard. Such a waste."

"But I didn't overhear anything," said Betty. "I was just walking down the street when I thought I saw somebody I knew walk out of this alley. I was trying to catch up to him when I ran into you."

"I wish I could believe you," answered the man pretending to be Martin. "But a reporter of your caliber just doesn't stumble upon two criminals discussing the details of the biggest crime of the century."

Betty's eyes lit up as her reporter's instincts kicked in. Reaching for her notepad and pencil, Betty asked, "Crime of the century, eh? Mind if I ask you a couple questions?"

The man sighed and gestured to the two figures behind her. "Gentlemen, please take care of this. Wait until I'm out of hearing range, however. I detest hearing a woman scream."

As the two thugs grabbed her, the man who looked like Martin moved past them and out of the alley. After waiting a few moments, one of the thugs asked, "Now, are you going to be a good girl and go nice and quiet? Or are you gonna make us hurt you?"

Stalling for time, Betty flashed her brightest smile and said, "Gee, boys, you aren't really going to hurt a lady now, are you? Why don't you take me out to dinner and we can talk about it?"

"Hah," laughed the thug standing behind her. "Yer a pretty thing, for sure, and funny, too. I'll make this as quick as possible." He placed one hand roughly over her mouth and wrapped the other one tightly around her throat. It happened so quickly, Betty never even had time to take a breath, much less scream.

Betty tried to struggle, but the two men were too strong, their grips too tight. She could feel her lungs burning already, and her vision was starting to blur. This was going to be quick, indeed.

Just as she was starting to black out, Betty heard a voice from the street yell, "Freeze! Let the woman go and put your hands up!"

The man holding her throat from behind her loosened his grip, but he didn't let go completely. She took a deep breath in through her nose, as his hand was still clamped over her mouth. The man in front of her holding her arms let her go, put his hands up in the air, and turned to face her savior.

Looking over the thug's shoulder, she saw it was Mick Finnley!

"Miss Dale, are you alright," Mick called out to her.

Betty felt the hand around her neck let go and heard the man rustling around beneath his coat. "Mick, he's got a gun," she tried to shout, but the words couldn't get past the hand over her mouth.

"Miss Dale," Mick called out again, but he was cut off by the loud crack of a gun. Betty heard Mick grunt as he lurched and fell to the ground.

Betty's panic quickly transformed into rage. Without the second man restraining her, Betty's arms were free. She swung her elbow with all of her might into the groin of the man behind her. He responded with a satisfying grunt, and his hand fell away from her face. Betty fell to her knees on the trash strewn ground of the alley. The other man turned in response to the commotion, and he reared back his hand to strike Betty. Reflexively, Betty reached for the nearest object on the ground. As the man's fist came crashing down, it was a steel trash can lid he struck. He screamed and cradled his broken hand to his chest.

Betty saw her chance to escape! She made a break for the street, but a hand reached out and grabbed her ankle. She screamed as she again fell to her knees. She turned just in time to see the pistol grip of a gun being swung at her head. She flinched, but it was too late. The butt of the gun struck her in the temple, and she lost consciousness.

"Miss Dale," came a voice from very far away. "Miss Dale, are you okay?" Closer now. Betty's eyes fluttered open to see the face of Detective Burks hovering over her.

"How is... oh, my." The pain in Betty's head almost overwhelmed her, but she focused on the single gunshot she had heard. "How is Mick?"

"Miss Dale, are you okay?"

"Officer Finnley is being loaded into the ambulance right now," said Burks. He took a bullet to the shoulder, but he should pull through."

Betty looked around and saw the two thugs lying unconscious. "What happened here?"

"Well, Miss Dale," answered Burks, "I was hoping you could tell me that. I sent Officer Finnley to follow our friend Renard, and shortly after, we get calls of a gunshot just blocks away from the hospital. We came here to find this mess. After you get checked out back at the hospital, I think you should answer some questions for us."

"Of... of course, Detective."

Burks put his arm under her shoulder and helped her to her feet. After she straightened up, Burks handed her something.

"Your umbrella, I assume?"

Betty stared down at the broken umbrella in her hands, and then over at the two thugs being handcuffed. "Uh, yes. Yes it is."

Harvey Bates smashed another cigarette butt out in the already over-flowing ashtray on his desk. Before the remains of the butt had even stopped smoldering, Harvey had already mindlessly reached into the pack to grab another cigarette.

This week was getting worse by the day! First, Bob Phillips, one of his longest-tenured operatives, fails to report in, then, Secret Agent X, his long-time boss and friend, gets captured by the police. What else could possibly go wrong?

One of the phones on Bates' desk started ringing, and he immediately regretted asking that question. Harvey checked his watch and saw that it was after seven o'clock at night, so he grabbed the evening edition of the newspaper and flipped to the Arts section.

"Colonial Research Foundation, Bates speaking," he said as he answered the phone.

"There's an interesting article in the Arts section this evening," said a woman's voice on the other end.

"I have it right here in front of me," replied Harvey. "Go ahead."

"Day code: 'Blue', 'Marked', 'Dancer'," said the woman.

Harvey started counted the words in the article and circled three that occurred at certain intervals. "Blue, Marked, Dancer, check. Sorry for the delay, Betty. What's going on?"

"Oh, Harvey, it's been just an awful day! Have you been keeping up with the news today?"

"Only what I've heard on the radio and read in the paper. I am aware of a certain individual being detained by the police, but the details I've been able to weed out have been scant. I had an operative working the same case, but he hasn't reported in for a couple of days now."

"I think I might have some info for you, Harvey," said Betty, her voice clearly shaken. She sounded exhausted.

"First, I can confirm that our employer is indeed in police custody. He is in the intensive care unit at Memorial Hospital under constant armed guard. I visited him myself."

Relief flooded over Harvey. "You saw him? How is he," he asked. "I'm sure he's already making plans to escape."

"It's not good, Harvey," said Betty. "He's in a coma and pretty beat up. The doctors are unsure if he will ever wake up again!" He could hear more than just exhaustion in her voice now; she was barely able to contain her grief.

"Don't worry, Betty," comforted Harvey. "Boss has been in worse pickles than this, I'm sure. Why, I wouldn't be surprised if this weren't all some elaborate ruse on his part." Harvey wished he were as confident as he was trying to sound for Betty's sake. "What else have you got?"

"You're right, Harvey," replied Betty. "Okay, next is a Frenchman named Sebastian Renard. He's the one who pulled our employer from the burning building. But he's involved in this deeper than just that."

Harvey glanced at the case file sitting on his desk. "Yeah, he's definitely one of the bad guys, Betty. I'd stay away from him if I were you. Wherever he goes, trouble follows."

"Oh, don't I know it," said Betty. "I just spent the past couple of hours at the hospital and then being interrogated by our friend Detective Burks. All because I was tailing Renard."

"Are you okay?" asked Harvey, suddenly worried.

"I'm fine, just a nasty bump on the head," said Betty. "Harvey, these guys are planning something big! I overheard Renard and a German fellow, and whatever they have planned is going down tomorrow night."

"What German guy?" asked Harvey, almost afraid to hear the answer.

"I have no idea who he really is," answered Betty, "but he was disguised as A.J. Martin. He looked just like him, Harvey! What is going on here?"

Harvey's worst fears were confirmed: Agent Loki was here! His presence in the city meant that this just got far more urgent. Whatever it was

Loki had planned was nearing its endgame, and with Secret Agent X out of the picture, it was up to them to stop him.

"Okay, Betty, I'm on it. Don't worry, we won't let the boss down!"

"I hope not," said Betty quietly. "Good night, Harvey. And good luck."

After Betty hung up, Harvey reached for his Wheeldex and opened it to the 'H' section. Flipping through the cards, he found the name he wanted and dialed the number on his phone. After a few rings, someone answered.

"Hobart Detective Agency," said the voice on the other end.

"Mr. Hobart, please," said Harvey. "I have an urgent need for his services."

Jim Hobart sat in his car and took another sip of his cold coffee. It was the middle of the night, and he had already put in a long day before he received the phone call. Hobart didn't normally drop a case he was working on to take on another, but this call came from his number one client. Tired or not, he wasn't going to refuse.

Hobart was staking out this particular alley in this particular industrial part of town strictly on a hunch. To be honest, his client didn't really provide much information, so a hunch was all he had to go on. But he felt pretty sure that the man he was looking for would be coming here sometime tonight. Or this morning, since it was now well past midnight.

The block just down the street was still cordoned off by the police; they were still investigating the fire at the chemical factory that was owned, in part, by his client. Hobart wasn't able to get anywhere near the factory, but he didn't think the man he was looking for would be returning there anyway. But in the alley across the street, now, that was something entirely different.

The car parked in that alley had been sitting there for at least a couple of days. Hobart had noticed the thin layer of spotty dirt on the windshield that had been left behind by the rainstorms that had been blowing through the city. No one had bothered to run the windshield wipers while the car was getting rained on, meaning the car had been parked here the whole time.

Hobart didn't have to wait long to congratulate himself. A few minutes after he finished his stale coffee, a lone figure came strolling down the street in front of him. His once-white suit was covered in soot, and his left arm hung in a sling. A perfect match for the description he was given.

And sure enough, the man quickly disappeared down the alley the car was sitting in.

A minute later, Hobart saw the car pull out of the alley with its headlights off. After turning on the street, the car's lights came on and his target drove off. The private investigator followed suit, pulling out onto the street and heading off in the direction the other car had driven.

Hobart knew to stay back a bit to not alert his target that he was being followed. Curiously, the car that was now following Hobart wasn't being quite so careful. Hobart checked his mirrors occasionally, and the car was definitely tailing him. Interesting.

As Hobart turned his eyes back to the road in front of him, he saw another car cut between his car and Renard's. So now Renard had a tail, too? This was turning into a parade.

The car following Renard was just as sloppy as the one on Hobart's tail, and it didn't take long for Renard to notice that he had company. The tires on Renard's car squealed as he made a sudden turn and accelerated. The car tailing Renard managed to make the turn, but lost a hub cap in the process as the driver ran the car up over the curb.

No longer needing to be subtle, Hobart stomped on the gas pedal and he, too, squealed his tires making the tight turn. Sure enough, the car behind him also sped up. The chase was on! But who was chasing whom?

The car ahead of him had regained control and was now right on Renard's bumper. Renard, in turn, was making more dangerous maneuvers in an attempt to shake his pursuer. To his credit, the driver chasing Renard managed to match him move for move.

Hobart had some experience in high-speed chases from his days as a cop, so he was able to keep up. The driver behind him wasn't fairing nearly as well, however, and was losing control on almost every turn now. It wouldn't be long before his pursuer would have to beg off or risk a high speed wreck.

The cars up front were playing bumper tag now. The pursuer was attempting to force Renard's car into a spin by ramming into the rear corner of his car. Renard was maintaining control for the moment, but he was fishtailing with each impact. Hobart had to brake a couple times to avoid smashing into the car in front of him.

Hobart lost his tail while going around the next corner. The poor mook behind the wheel of that car just couldn't make the corner at the speed they were traveling. Instead, he maintained a straight line in the direction he was already going. Now, Hobart could concentrate on the car in front of him. Renard was a bad guy, but he was Hobart's bad guy!

Just then, the car in front of him slammed into Renard's right rear and succeeded in spinning him out. Impressively, Renard controlled the spin and turned it into a right turn. Renard's pursuer couldn't maintain control, however, and he spun out completely. Hobart was just quick enough to make the turn Renard had taken. Now it was just the two of them.

Renard was maintaining a straight course, and was slightly pulling away from Hobart. The P.I. realized Renard had the faster car, so unless something drastic happened, he would eventually leave Hobart in the dust.

Luckily for Hobart, something drastic was about to happen. He glanced out his side window and saw the car that had been pursuing him now running a perpendicular course to the one he and Renard were on. At this rate of speed, there was no way for Renard to avoid being hit. Hobart slammed on his brakes to avoid being tangled up in the wreck that was about to explode in front of him.

With a horrendous noise of crunching metal and shattering glass, Renard's car was struck heavily just behind the passenger side door. The car that hit Renard bore the brunt of the impact directly to the front, and Hobart saw at least one person thrown from that car through the windshield. Hobart felt sorry for the guy.

Hobart managed to come to a stop a few feet away from the smoldering mass of twisted metal. He saw Renard crawl out of the driver's side door and stumble a bit before managing to catch his balance. He was obviously shaken, but he appeared to be okay. The driver of the other car was in worse shape, but Hobart could see him moving. The man on the pavement was trying to crawl off the road, but his legs weren't cooperating very well. As he was rushing to the aid of the man on the ground, two more men spilled out of the back doors.

Just then, the other car came screeching to a stop from the other direction, and four more men jumped out onto the street to join the party. Hobart instinctively dropped into a defensive posture and started backing up. He came to an abrupt stop in the center of the intersection when his back met the back of who he assumed was Sebastian Renard.

"I do not know who you are, *Monsieur*," said the Frenchman, "but it appears we are in the same predicament, no?"

"So it would seem," replied Hobart. "I sure hope you're better in a fight than you are behind the wheel of a car."

"Oho, my new friend has a sharp tongue!"

The six men were circling around them. One of them shouted out, "Hey, Frenchie! We got a bone to pick with you. Seems like you hired a bunch of our pals to help you out, only most of them got dead or thrown in jail. We're gonna make you pay for that!"

With that, the six men moved in for the kill. Oddly, none of them seemed to be brandishing a weapon of any sort. Hobart figured it would be much quicker and more efficient to simply mow the two of them down with bullets. Not that he was complaining.

The attackers' numbers initially seemed to work against them; they couldn't help getting in each other's way. "You're all a little too eager, gents," said Hobart between fending off punches. "It would be much easier if you lined up and took your beatings one at a time!"

The P.I. ducked one man's punch that ended up contacting another thug in the face. Hobart responded with a punch of his own to the original attacker's gut. That man stumbled back into the third attacker, giving Hobart a second to catch his breath. He glanced over his shoulder to see how his ally was holding up, and he was shocked to see the Frenchman deftly handling his attackers with blows from his fists and feet. All three thugs were soon backing off and nursing wounds.

Hobart's attention was quickly drawn back to his own attackers when he saw a fist coming at him from the corner of his eye. He reacted, but not quite quickly enough, and the blow glanced off of his brow. He was knocked back into Renard, and the two men's feet got tangled. Renard managed to keep his balance, but Hobart fell hard to the ground.

Hobart felt Renard's leg swing over his head in a powerful roundhouse kick, and Renard's foot smashed into the side of the thug's head. One down, five more to go.

Before he could get to his feet, the remaining thugs moved in again, except this time they were coordinating their attacks. Renard managed to keep two of the men at bay, but two more attacked him from behind. Hobart couldn't help, as he was struggling to regain his feet while fending off the last thug.

While three of the attackers occupied Renard, the fourth turned back to Hobart and grabbed him from behind. The other thug was now raining punches down on the defenseless P.I.

Barely holding onto consciousness, Hobart suddenly felt the sharp pain of a blade pricking his throat.

"Hey Renard," called out the thug holding the knife to Hobart's throat, "give up or I give yer buddy here a second smile."

Renard hesitated and turned around slightly to assess the situation. Hobart saw something in the stranger's eyes that he wasn't expecting.

More than just empathy, Renard showed genuine concern for Hobart's predicament.

"Alas, *mon ami*, I cannot let them kill you." Renard put up his hands and put his head down. He was instantly tackled to the ground.

As Hobart was dragged back towards one of the cars, he watched helplessly as Renard was first beaten, then bound, and finally blindfolded. Shortly thereafter, Hobart shared the same fate, and the night sky disappeared behind a thick piece of cloth.

Harvey Bates opened the door to the darkened room. He flipped on a switch, and a lone naked bulb hanging from the ceiling gave off a weak circle of light. A man sat hunched over in a chair with his hands tied around his back. Blood from his beaten face dripped onto his once-white suit, mixing with the dirt and soot that stained it.

Harvey's operatives had worked him over pretty good, almost too good. But he couldn't really blame them. Two of their partners were in the hospital after tonight's action, after all. Harvey had a personal bone to pick with this guy, as he was the one ultimately responsible for Secret Agent X getting captured.

As Harvey approached Renard, the man lifted his head and looked directly into Harvey's eyes. A look of shock and relief spread over the man's face, and he threw his head back and began to laugh.

This was not the reaction Harvey was expecting. "Care to let me in on the joke, Renard?"

"*Oui, mon ami*," said the Frenchman, still chuckling. The man's voice then changed to something more familiar. "Harvey Bates, you magnificent bastard! You can't imagine how happy I am to see you! Now, if you don't mind, untie me. My arm really hurts."

Harvey's blood ran cold as he instantly recognized the man's voice. But there's no way that this was possible... except, of course it was possible! If anyone could have pulled this off, it was him!

"Boss!?" Harvey was still unsure. "Boss, is that you?" Harvey reached behind the chair and undid the knot binding the man's hands.

The man reached up to his face and began peeling away his skin. He ripped away the bottom half of what turned out to be a mask. "Yes, Harvey, it's me," he said, his voice gaining strength. "It's Secret Agent X!"

Secret Agent X felt like a new man. Despite the bruises he'd acquired the night before and the complete lack of sleep over the past few days, the warm shower he just took greatly improved his attitude.

While it felt good to have his own face on for a bit after almost three straight days wearing the same mask, it was time to pull out his disguise kit one more time. The face he chose to wear today was one he was he was very familiar with, so he applied it with practiced ease.

The adjoining room of the safe house held a kitchenette, and he could smell the breakfast Harvey Bates was cooking up for them. As Agent X walked in to join him, Harvey looked up from the stove.

"Why, if it isn't A.J. Martin, famous news reporter," joked Harvey. After giving him an appraising look, Harvey added, "Gee, boss, you look a heck of a lot better than you did last night."

"No thanks to you and your boys, Harvey," replied Agent X while taking a seat at the table. "You guys worked me over pretty good."

"Yeah, uh, about that..." Harvey began, hanging his head in shame. "We didn't know it was you, boss, honest. The plan was to have Hobart track down Renard, then snatch him away while pretending to be disgruntled mob goons. You know, for Jim's sake. We don't want to clue him in on our operations. After that, we were just going to beat Renard until he spilled Loki's plans."

"Don't worry about it, Harvey," said Secret Agent X, "you were only doing your job. I certainly can't be mad at you for beating me up while trying to rescue me, now can I?"

"Um... no?"

Agent X laughed, and said, "I promised you I would answer all your questions, Harvey, so let's talk while we eat."

Harvey brought some scrambled eggs over and joined X at the table.

"Well, let's start with the first thing, boss," said Harvey. "How did Loki and his goons catch on to you so quickly? They have a lot of intel on you, that's no joke."

"And every bit of it is information I slowly leaked to them over the past few months," answered Agent X. "When we caught wind of Loki's agents sniffing around, I decided to give them some tasty tidbits. They did manage to piece a lot more together than I expected them to, however. That caught me a bit off guard. I had to revise my plan on the fly a few times to keep one step ahead of them."

"So who is it the police have locked up in the hospital?" Before Agent X could answer, Harvey put the dots together and snapped his fingers. "Renard! The real one."

"Of course. When I regained consciousness in the remains of the burned out warehouse, I found him badly burned but still alive. I quickly put a little make up on him before fleeing the scene."

"So that Burks would naturally assume it was you."

"Bingo." Agent X looked at his friend, reflecting on the events of the past few days. "These Germans are extremely clever, Harvey. We can't underestimate them for a second."

"And what is it they are after, exactly?" asked Harvey around a mouthful of eggs.

"That's something that took me a while to figure out myself," said X. "At first I thought I was the primary target. But as it turns out, eliminating me was just one part of their plan. No, what they were after, exactly, is the secret formula to my masks."

"Wait a minute," said Harvey incredulously, "this is all over some make-up?"

"Oh, they're much more than just that," said Secret Agent X. "When properly formulated, my putty creates a life-like second skin. With a skilled application, someone wearing one of these masks could pass any close examination except, maybe, for one done by a doctor. Why, I can mimic almost anybody well enough to fool their own mother."

"But what does Loki plan to do with it," asked Harvey.

"That's what worries me, Harvey. I haven't figured that out yet."

Secret Agent X walked into the crowded press room at City Hall. Interestingly, it was the President's Press Secretary that was preparing to give this press conference.

"A.J. Martin! You're a busy man today," came a loud voice from a hefty reporter in his typically-wrinkled brown suit.

"Sam Webber," Agent X called back in A.J. Martin's distinctive voice, "how are ya, pal? And what the heck are you talking about?"

"Didn't you just leave this dance, A.J.," asked Sam. "I could swear I just saw you walking outta here a few minutes ago with Betty on your arm."

Not enough sleep and too many blows to the head over the past few days made thinking clearly a bit difficult for a moment. Agent X tried to piece together what Sam was talking about when it all suddenly became chillingly coherent.

"Sam, this is going to sound very odd, but please answer me as clearly as possible," said Agent X, no longer smiling. "What time was it when Betty and I left?"

"Why, it was just about 20 minutes ago, A.J.," replied Sam. "I was surprised you two would be leaving before the Press Secretary's announcement."

Agent X was turning to leave when he paused for a moment and looked back at Sam. "What announcement, Sam? What's going on with the President?"

Sam took his cigar out of his mouth and leaned in towards Agent X. "Word has it," he said quietly, "that the President has been invited to a dinner by some visiting dignitaries."

Secret Agent X grabbed Sam by the shoulders. "Which dignitaries, Sam? Where is the dinner going to be held?"

"The Germans. On board their airship, the *Gotterdammerung*," replied Sam. "A.J. what's going on? Why are you acting so strange?"

"Never you mind, Sam," said Agent X. "You'll have to read my story to find out!" Agent X wished he really felt as flippant as he was pretending to be. He made his way through the crowd toward the exit.

Agent X rushed out of the room and over to the nearest bank of pay phones. He quickly dialed in a number and tapped his fingers impatiently on the booth until someone picked up on the other end.

"Harvey, I have no time to explain," said Agent X. "Just grab whoever you can and meet me at the airfield where the *Gotterdammerung* is moored right away! I know what—or who—Loki is after now, and he's on that airship. And Loki's got Betty, too!"

Secret Agent X had been waiting for just a few minutes, but time was quickly slipping away. The thunderstorm rolling in would soon make any air travel impossible. He peered at the hanger again, and the doors were still closed. They still had some time left, but not much.

He soon saw the headlights of a car cutting through the rain off in the distance. The headlights turned off as the car approached Agent X, and after the car pulled to a stop, Harvey Bates and three of his men got out.

"Sorry, Boss, these are all the guys I had with me," said Harvey. "What have we got?"

Agent X pointed back to the hangar he had been watching. "Loki and his men are over there," said Agent X. "I'm guessing they'll be leaving shortly, so we need to get down there right away if we're going to stop them."

No sooner had Secret Agent X said this when the doors of the hangar began to open. Several men pushed an airplane out of the hangar and into the light rain that had started. The plane was a two-seater with an unusual contraption attached to the top wing. The attachment appeared to be a large hook, something that Agent X had never seen before.

Following the plane out of the hangar came Agent Loki, and behind him were two rather large men, one leading an equally large German Shepard dog on a leash. Between them walked Betty Dale, her hands bound in front of her. All told, X counted a dozen enemies.

"Boss, we're outnumbered better than two to one," said Harvey.

"Good," responded Agent X with a grin, "I was beginning to think this would be difficult."

"All right, boys," said Harvey to his men, "get ready. We'll move in behind them and take the bigger guys out first."

"And no guns," added Secret Agent X, "We can't risk Miss Dale getting hurt. In fact, leave those two with the dog and Loki to me."

While three of the men were occupied with starting the plane's engine, Agent X and his men moved around the back of the hangar and snuck up behind the unsuspecting Germans.

Agent X reached the plane just as Betty was being strapped into the rear passenger seat by one of the ground crew. Agent Loki, wearing the same A.J. Martin face as Secret Agent X, spotted him first.

"*Achtung!* Behind you, fools," shouted Loki. The two large henchmen turned at the same time to confront Agent X. To their credit, neither was caught off guard. One dropped instantly into defensive posture, while the other one released his dog, pointing at Agent X and ordering it to attack.

Rather than attempt to fend off the charging dog, Agent X calmly held his hand out towards the animal and stared into its eyes. After a moment of eye contact, the dog instantly went from a snarling beast to sitting obediently just inches away from Secret Agent X's outstretched hand. With a sharp whistle and a gesture back at the pair of Germans, Agent X sent the dog back to attack its former masters.

The Germans had just a brief moment to glance at each other in confusion before the dog was upon them. The man still holding the dog's now-unoccupied leash in his hand went down screaming. The other man avoided his partner's fate, but now faced Secret Agent X alone.

The man was good in a fight. Agent X would give him that. He was

...the attachment appeared to be a large hook..

able to fend of X's first few strikes, and even managed to throw a return punch of his own. Agent X deftly sidestepped the punch, however, and grabbed the man's arm between his own. With one swift twist, the man's arm broke with a sickening crack.

Agent X flung the screaming man to the ground and turned to see Loki climbing into the cockpit. Scrambling up the side of the aircraft, X grabbed Loki from behind and pulled him down off the plane. Both men tumbled to the rain-soaked ground in a heap. They scrambled to their feet, dripping wet, and stood face to identical face.

"*Was ist das*," asked a confused German. He looked back and forth between the two A.J.s, unsure of which one to point his gun at.

"Shoot him, you fool," yelled Agent Loki, pointing at Secret Agent X. The barrel of the gun swiveled to point at X.

"Not me, you fool," yelled Agent X in return, "Shoot him!"

Before the confused man could decide which A.J. Miller to shoot, he was struck from behind with a large wrench. In his place now stood Harvey Bates, who found himself facing the same dilemma that had flustered the German. "Boss?"

Secret Agent X looked over at Loki and noticed something was seriously wrong with his face. The A.J. Martin mask was starting to warp and bubble, and soon smoke began to rise from it. Agent Loki suddenly screamed in pain and reached up and began clawing at his skin.

"Remember how I told you how I leaked that information to Loki's agents, Harvey," said Agent X. "Not all of it was entirely accurate. The final key component to the face putty was intentionally incorrect. Instead, I gave them a similar component, but one that has a rather nasty reaction to water."

Loki looked up at Agent X, and for the first time, X saw the enemy agent's true face. He noted the gruesome scar running down Loki's right cheek. This man was indeed a master of disguise if he could hide that so well!

"Fools," snarled Loki, not yet beaten. He stomped his heel into the puddle at his feet and twisted his foot. X looked down and saw that he and Harvey were standing in the same puddle.

"Harvey, look...," he began, but he was cut off when jolt of electricity coursed through his body. Harvey, too, was shocked, and both men were knocked off their feet. The jolt ended as quickly as it began, but fireworks were still running up and down Secret Agent X's nerves.

Both Agent X and Harvey struggled to their feet, but it was too late. Loki was in the cockpit of the plane moving towards the runway. X made to run after the plane, hoping to catch up with it before it got up to speed, but his nervous system was still haywire and his legs refused to cooperate. He fell to his knees in the mud, and he watched in futility as the plane bounced down the runway and took off.

The powerful winds and stinging rain made for a bumpy ride, but Harvey Bates had managed to keep the ancient Curtis Jenny airborne—so far. They had found the dilapidated plane in the back of the hangar, and X could barely make out the name "Dave Stevens Flying Circus" in faded paint on the fuselage. It had taken precious minutes to fuel the plane and to get the engine started, but the tough old bird had still proven airworthy.

Agent X tapped on Harvey's shoulder in front of him and pointed to the two o'clock position. Off in the distance, coming out from behind a cloud, were the lights of what could only be an enormous aircraft. The *Gotterdammerung* was eight hundred feet long if it was an inch, and judging by the lights, they were just a little over a mile away. Harvey gave Secret Agent X a thumbs up and steered the plane towards the airship.

As they got closer, Agent X saw a plane suspended from beneath the *Gotterdammerung*. So that's what the structure on the top wing was for: a skyhook to dock with the mother ship. The plane was being winched up into a hangar bay, and Agent X watched helplessly as the bay doors slammed closed.

"What now?" Harvey yelled over his shoulder.

"Get me up to the command car," Agent X yelled back, pointing to the train car-sized gondoal hanging from the nose of the airship.

"And then what?" asked Harvey. "You gonna just knock on the door?"

"Precisely," responded X with a smile. He reached down and unlatched his safety belt and climbed up onto his seat. Grabbing the top wing spar, he hoisted himself out of the cockpit and climbed onto the top wing.

"Boss! What are you doing?" screamed Harvey while looking back over his shoulder at the now-empty passenger seat.

Secret Agent X swung his head down over the front of the wing so he was face to face with Harvey when the pilot turned back around.

"Gah!" Harvey screamed in surprise. Had he not had goggles on, his eyes might very well bugged right out of his head.

"Just get me up to that wheel well, Harvey, and I'll handle the rest," said Agent X.

That task was easier said than done, since the winds were now buffeting both the airship and the plane fiercely. But Harvey managed to get the top wing of the plane to within arm's reach of the wheel hanging off the bottom of the command car. Without a second thought, Agent X leaped, and just managed to grab the strut of the wheel.

Hanging by one arm, Agent X looked back to see Harvey trying to maintain his altitude just below the command car. The wind was getting too dangerous for the little plane, so X waved Harvey off. Harvey waggled his wings to confirm he understood, then banked his wings and peeled away.

Using various pieces of the gondola's structure as handholds, Secret Agent X made his way across the car's undercarriage towards the side where the door was. The strong winds made grasping the rain-slicked metal quite difficult, and more than once Agent X was sure that he was going to lose his grip and fall a thousand feet to his doom. When he did eventually make it to the side, he pulled on the swing-out steps and hoisted himself up.

Standing on the small step and grasping the safety handle, Agent X used his free hand to rap on the door. He then ducked down below the level of the window, as not to be seen. Moments later, the window opened and the head of a very confused German airman peeked out. X slammed the heel of his hand into the man's nose, knocking him back away from the door. Before any of the shocked airmen inside the command bridge could react, he reached in through the open window and opened the door.

Agent X stepped in through the open door and faced the lone officer in the command bridge. "Permission to come aboard, *Herr Kapitan*?" said Agent X.

The dumbfounded officer stared at Secret Agent X for a brief moment, then turned back to yelling orders at the crewmen on the bridge. Now it was Agent X's turn to be surprised. After his violent entrance, X was fully prepared to defend himself and fight his way to the airship itself. Instead he was being largely ignored as the crew frantically scrambled around him. Even the airman he had struck on his way in had clambered back to his feet and was working at an instrument panel.

An instant later revealed what the crew was so preoccupied with. A huge wall of air slammed into the side of the *Gotterdammerung* and the entire airship lurched to starboard. Almost simultaneously, the bow of the airship pitched downward at an alarmingly steep angle as a powerful downdraft came crashing down from thousands of feet above. The crew had no time for Agent X because they were desperately struggling to save the airship from a raging thunderstorm!

"Release the ballast," screamed the captain to the crewman Agent X had just bloodied, "Release all of it, empty the tanks!"

As the water ballast tanks were emptied, the plunging airship slowly righted itself and leveled out. Before any of the crewmen could turn their attention to him, Secret Agent X made a break for the room at the back of the command car that contained the ladder to the airship. The radioman made a lunge at Agent X as he passed through the navigation room, but X sidestepped the attack. Looping his arm around his attacker's, Agent X used the man's momentum against him and sent him flying back through the doorway to the bridge, temporarily cutting off any pursuit from the rest of the aircrew. X then rushed through the doorway leading to the back utility room and scrambled up the ladder.

Secret Agent X moved as quickly as he could along the catwalk through the airship's superstructure. He held tightly onto the rope safety rail as the airship was knocked back and forth by the strong winds. The forest of interlocking girders that made up the airship's framework creaked and groaned as the ship was twisted and stressed to the very edge of the its structural limits. He could hear the last remnants of the ballast water sloshing around in the ballast tanks on either side of the catwalk, and the enormous gasbags that filled the majority of the ship's airframe billowed ominously overhead. Despite the best efforts of the captain and aircrew, Secret Agent X wasn't very optimistic about the chances of the *Gotterdammerung* surviving the storm.

After what seemed like an eternity, Agent X managed to cross the hundred or so feet that separated the command bridge from the passenger section. Time was quickly running out, and he still had to find both the President and Betty! The door from the catwalk entered into the lower deck of the passenger section. Remembering the airship schematics, he knew this deck held the crew quarters and kitchen. They wouldn't likely be down here, so he bounded up the stairs to the main deck.

At the top of the stairs, Agent X was faced with three doors. In front of him, the door was marked "Passenger Cabins", the door to the left "Private", and to the right was "Dining Room". The formal dinner would be in the dining room, so that's where the President would be. Finding Betty would have to wait.

Agent X entered the dining room just as the *Gotterdammerung* again lurched violently. Diners were flung screaming out of their chairs and dishes flew off the tables and shattered on the floor. X regained his footing and looked down the fifty-foot-long room. Several smaller tables were situated around the main table, which is where he saw the President seated. The President had been able to maintain his seat, but the two Secret Service agents flanking him had both fallen to the floor.

"Mr. President, I think it's time you left, sir," said Agent X as he approached the three of them. "You are in grave danger as long as you stay aboard this ship."

"Young man, I..." the President began to say, but he was interrupted as two of the German officers at the table drew their dress uniform sabers. The blades looked more functional than mere props, and appeared decidedly lethal.

"You won't be going anywhere," snarled one of the fake diplomats. "Loki has plans for you!"

Secret Agent X and one of the Secret Service men exchanged a quick glance, then both men sprang into action. X kicked a plate that was teetering on the edge of the table into the face of one of the Germans, and he quickly followed up with a lunge at for the man's sword. The plate full of food gave Agent X all the distraction he needed, and he was able to grab the man's forearm. With a sharp twist, the German's elbow was hyperextended, and his sword belonged to Agent X.

Looking around, Agent X saw the Secret Service agent grappling with the other German against the railing in front of the observation deck. The airship gave another sudden jolt, and both men were thrown into the outward-slanting window pane. The glass shattered under the impact, and they disappeared into the gray maelstrom raging outside.

Panic gripped the dining room. Agent X wasn't sure how many of the Germans were actually working for Loki, but his main concern now was getting the President off the *Gotterdammerung.*

Grabbing the remaining Secret Service agent, Agent X asked, "Can you fly a plane?"

"Yes, sir," he responded, "I flew combat missions during the war."

"Good," said Agent X. "We need to make for the hangar bay. We need to get the President safely off this airship."

Turning to the President, Agent X said, "Forgive me, sir, I need to know." He then reached up and gave the President's face a pinch and a twist. The President yelped with pain, but his skin didn't peel off. "Just had to be sure," said Agent X.

As they made for the door, the ship pitched sharply upward and began to ascend. This was the endgame, then! That fool of a captain had doomed his ship when he released all the ballast. The Zeppelin was now caught in the powerful updraft at the heart of the thunderstorm, and X knew that the airship would be carried thousands of feet up into the atmosphere before being torn to pieces.

As they struggled along the catwalk towards the hanger bay amidships, Secret Agent X could see two planes hanging above the closed hangar. A figure was climbing down from one of the planes, and Agent X caught a glimpse of blonde hair on another figure already in the passenger seat. Betty!

Agent X threw caution to the wind and raced the remaining distance along the catwalk to the launch platform. The man wearing a German officer's dress uniform turned away from the instrument panel to face him. The scar on his face revealed the man's true identity.

"Secret Agent X," hissed Loki as he drew his sword. "None of you shall escape here alive!"

As the two men crossed swords in the middle of the launch platform, the *Gotterdammerung* shuddered around them. Loud cracking now drowned out the sound of the groaning airframe as the interlocking support girders began to snap throughout the airship.

Both combatants circled each other on the pitching platform, exchanging strikes while trying to maintain their balance. Agent X was holding his own for the moment, but he quickly surmised that Loki's swordsmanship outmatched his own. He could hold Loki off for a while, but would it be long enough?

"Give it up, Agent X," snarled Loki as he backed X into the platform's instrument panel. "I am clearly the superior swordsman. I can still save your precious Betty if you would quit being such a nuisance!"

Agent X glanced over Loki's shoulder and saw that the President and his Secret Service man had boarded their plane and had the engine running. A particularly violent shudder of the ship separated both combatants, and X took the opportunity to catch his breath and smile at Loki.

"You clearly are the better swordsman," said Agent X, "but I haven't been completely honest with you."

Loki hesitated. "What do you mean," he asked.

"I am ambidextrous," said Agent X as he flipped his sword over to his left hand. X was satisfied to see a look of uncertainty cross Loki's face. Secret Agent X reached behind him with his right hand and flipped the switch to open the hangar door.

Now on the attack, Agent X started raining blows on Loki, driving him back across the platform. "I noticed from your scar and from your fencing style that you have one weakness," said Agent X around sword strokes. "You may be a master when fighting a right-handed opponent, but you are vulnerable when defending against a south paw!" Out of the corner of his eye, X saw the plane carrying the President drop through the open bay door. Now to reach Betty!

Just then, the overtaxed airframe of the *Gotterdammerung* finally gave up the battle against the thunderstorm in a spectacular fashion. With a deafening roar, the airship's steel frame tore asunder, sending metal fragments flying through the air. The enormous gas cells ripped open, and stray sparks from the shearing metal ignited the escaping gas. The resulting fireball engulfed the front half of the airship in a matter of seconds. The dying airship broke in two, and the hanger deck amidships was ground zero.

Agent X leaped for a swinging girder as the launch platform fell away with the burning front half of the airship. He looked down to see Loki shaking his fist at him in rage as the flaming wreck of the airship's bow sank into the clouds below.

The stern half's gas cells were still momentarily intact but the remaining airframe was now spinning out of control, completely at the mercy of the thunderstorm. Agent X watched in horror as the plane containing Betty was thrown from what remained of the hangar bay. Without a second thought, X let go of the girder and dove after the plane.

The powerful winds tore at his skin and clothes, but Secret Agent X pressed his arms to his side and pointed himself at the falling plane. The same winds that were buffeting X were also slamming into the plane's wings, miraculously giving the plane some lift. His streamlined form gave Agent X far less wind resistance, and after free falling for several seconds, he crashed directly into one of the plane's upper wings. Despite the wind shear, he eventually managed to position himself above the cockpit and swing himself down into the pilot's seat.

"Going somewhere, Miss Dale," he shouted over his shoulder as he tried to start up the plane's engine.

"Just get us out of here, Secret Agent X!" Betty screamed in response.

"As you wish, Betty." The engine started with a roar, and after plummeting hundreds of feet, Agent X managed to level out the plane.

After escaping the ravages of the thunderstorm, the plane ride back to the airstrip proved to be relatively pleasant. The storm still raged in the distance, but it was moving quickly eastward and had already passed over the city.

"Look, up ahead," said Betty as she pointed towards the lights of the airfield. "It looks like the other plane made it out of the storm, as well."

Agent X watched as the other plane approached the runway and landed safely. He circled around the airfield, looking for the old "Stevens Flying Circus" plane. He saw that it, too, had survived the storm. He waggled his wings at the crowd below and then flew off towards the west.

"Where are we going?" asked Betty.

"Ah, *Mademoiselle*," said Secret Agent X in Renard's French accent, "I believe I promised to fly away with you and live happily ever after."

"You wouldn't...," said Betty, a hint of hope at the edge of her voice.

"You're right, I wouldn't," said Agent X in his own voice. "I'm flying us to a private airstrip. I would rather avoid the circus of law enforcement and press that will be greeting the President back there. Prying questions, and all that. I'll have Harvey pick us up from there."

"Oh, X," said Betty, obviously disappointed.

"One day, Betty" laughed Secret Agent X, "one day, I promise."

THE END

Meeting Agent "X"

Before writing this story for Airship 27, I had never heard of the character Secret Agent X. I discovered pulp heroes as a kid with the Golden Press Doc Savage reprints back in the 70s. (It wasn't until later that I realized that the Lone Ranger, Conan, Tarzan, and John Carter of Mars comics and stories I had been enjoying for years were contemporaries of old Doc.) From those roots, I found the Shadow, G-8, the Spider, and many others. But I never ran across Secret Agent X.

A couple years ago, a friend of mine talked me into joining him at PulpFest in my then-hometown of Columbus, Ohio. I gravitated towards the Airship 27 tables, mostly because of all the fantastic, colorful titles they had on display, but not inconsequentially because the two gentlemen manning the tables were extremely friendly. Long story short, after a very nice chat with Ron Fortier, some emails were exchanged, and I decided to try my hand at writing a New Pulp story for Airship 27.

I had my pick of any of the characters Airship 27 was currently publishing stories for. I was naturally attracted to both the Masked Rider and Ki-Gor of the Jungle due to their similarities to the Lone Ranger and Tarzan characters I loved and knew so well. But when Ron suggested Secret Agent X, I jumped at the chance. Not only was this a chance to help Ron fill a need (note to aspiring writers: being willing to provide a story that fits your editor's needs is always a good move), but writing a character that I was unfamiliar with would allow me to try something new and work out my creative muscles a bit.

So I immersed myself in the character. I purchased and read through all of the excellent Secret Agent X anthologies that Airship 27 published, and I researched the character as much as I could through the internet. I familiarized myself with the regular cast of characters and the style of the stories. I was all set to go!

Then I sat down to actually write the story, and that's when I realized that this wasn't going to be as easy as I thought.

Writing pulp stories isn't like writing any other type of fiction. Pulp writing looks deceptively simple (which is why many of the old pulp authors were looked down upon by more "literary" writers and publishers), but in reality, it's actually very difficult. Not only do you have to tell a satisfying story, but you have to do so while concentrating on action and adventure and while using expected character and genre tropes. That's a lot of balls to juggle.

On my first attempt at the story, not only did I drop all of those balls, they bounced away everywhere: under the desk, behind the couch, down the basement stairs. It was a disaster. So I had to regroup and start all over again.

My biggest challenges were using some of the character tropes effectively, using the supporting characters effectively, and creating an interesting villain. Secret Agent X's main gimmick is his ability to disguise himself as almost anyone. How do I do that in a way that hasn't been done before? And Agent X has a wonderful cast of supporting characters that fill diverse roles. But which ones should I use in my story, and how can I make them seem like more than just minions? And a great villain needs to challenge the hero more than ever before. How will the nemesis in my story push Agent X in new and exciting ways?

A timely conversation with fellow writer Jeff Venture helped save the day for me. Jeff made some suggestions and gently nudged me towards where I wanted my story to go. He helped me get all my juggling balls back up in the air, so to speak. Once I got that rhythm down I really started to have fun, and I was even able to toss a couple more balls into the mix.

I could have fiddled and rewritten the story til the cows came home, but I knew that at some point I would have to send my story off to Ron. I think I addressed the challenges of writing a Secret Agent X story as best as I could, and I know I had a lot of fun writing it. I will let you, the reader, judge how well I succeeded. I can only hope that you experience as much enjoyment reading the story as I had writing it.

ANDY FIX- first discovered heroes such as the Lone Ranger, Conan, Tarzan, John Carter, and Doc Savage as a child. Many years later, he would come to realize that all these characters originated in pulp magazines. Since then, Andy has been a fan of all things Pulp, and he is very excited to be writing New Pulp adventures.

Andy is currently working on an Air War story with friend and fellow New Pulp writer Jeff Venture. He is also in the early planning stages of a New Pulp novel featuring Sir Axel the Axe, Knight of the Round Table, an original character of Andy's creation.

For updates on these and Andy's other writing projects, you can follow him on Twitter (@AndyFixWriter) and on Facebook (facebook.com/Andyfixwriter).

SECRET AGENT "X"

Devil
in the
Deep Blue
Sea

by Fred Adams Jr.

13 October 1919

Midnight. Under a full moon, the British merchant vessel Raleigh plowed through the North Atlantic hauling a cargo of Manchester textiles to the United States. Her bow clove the waves like a scalpel as she followed her course through the cold autumn waters.

On watch, First Mate Robbie Crayton stared across leagues of silvered waves that rose and fell like the pulse of the universe. The October breeze was stiff and he pulled his knit cap over his ears. The mate raised binoculars to his eyes and scanned to the west. Nothing to see but the sea, he said to himself, laughing at his own joke. He turned to the east and what he saw froze his blood. Robbie had served in His Majesty's Navy in the Great War, and he knew that the approaching trail of bubbles could mean only one thing.

"Torpedo port aft!" he shouted and shouted again. By the time the helm answered, the torpedo struck, destroying the freighter's twin screws, shattering its rudder, and twisting its shafts, leaving the freighter dead in the water. Captain Shanks was already on the bridge when Robbie got there.

"The helm's not answering, Mister Crayton."

"We've been torpedoed, Sir," Crayton said. "I saw it coming just before it hit."

"A torpedo?" The captain turned to stare Crayton in the eye. "Are you mad?"

"A voice from behind them said, "If he is, then we all are, Captain. Look."

A sailor pointed through the port side windows of the bridge. A dark shape broke the surface.

"It's a U-boat," said Shanks.

"Not just any U-boat, Sir," said Crayton.

The men stared at the image painted on the conning tower, a great round eye encircled with lightning bolts. "Unless I'm mistaken," said Crayton, either that's a ghost or it's the Arges off our bow."

"Mister Crayton, send a distress call immediately." The mate ran from the wheelhouse. As Shanks watched, figures scrambled from the U-boat's forward hatch and manned its deck gun. Before a distress call could be sent, two well placed shots took down the Raleigh's wireless antenna. Shanks stared into the eye on the conning tower and realized he was staring into the unflinching eye of Death.

"Break out the arms," barked Shanks. "Call general quarters. Prepare to repel boarders."

The crew of the Raleigh fought the good fight, but their handful of carbines and pistols were no match for the machine guns of the submariners. In moments the battle was over and the attackers swarmed aboard. All wore the black leather jackets and peaked caps of the German Navy. Though they were capable and moved with military precision, there were few whole men among them. Some missed fingers, hands, eyes, ears. Some were badly scarred. Some walked with the stiffness of an artificial limb. But to a man they were purposeful and menacing.

The survivors of the gun battle were herded onto the foredeck. "This is an act of war," blurted Shanks, "and the war's been over for years." One of the U-boat crew drove his fist into the captain's jaw, knocking him to the deck. Before Shanks's men could move to defend their captain, a cold voice cut through the hiss of the waves and the rumble of the engines.

"Perhaps your war is over, Captain Shanks, but mine will never end." The boarders parted and a tall man dressed in the same leathers as the others stepped forward and grabbed Shanks by his collar, lifting him off the deck like a child and standing him on his feet. "I apologize for the rudeness of my men, Captain. A person of your rank deserves more respect."

Shanks stared into the speaker's face and gasped in spite of himself. One side of the face was that of a handsome blonde haired, blue eyed Aryan, the other was a dark mass of scar tissue like an unfinished sculpture in violet agate. A patch covered his ruined eye. "Koehler," said the disbelieving Shanks. "But you're…"

"Dead?" said Koehler. The right side of his face smiled and he let a mirthless chuckle escape his misshapen mouth. "As the Americans' Mark Twain once wrote, 'The report of my death was an exaggeration.' Yours, I fear may not be so."

Shanks's mind raced. They had nothing of value the submarine could carry in enough volume to be worth the effort. "If it's the ship you want, I'm afraid you'll have to tow her to dry dock before she's of any value."

Koehler's crooked smile turned up the corner of his mouth. "I have no need of the Raleigh nor of your cargo, Captain, nor of you." He turned to his men. "Put them off the ship."

The captain and remaining crew were marched down the deck at gun point and forced into a lifeboat. As they climbed in, Shanks saw to his horror that the oars were missing. "You can't just set us adrift. This boat has no oars."

Again that disconcerting half-smile. "You will have no need of them,

Captain." And over the protesting shouts of Shanks and his men, Koehler gave the command: "Lower away."

As the lifeboat bobbed on the waves, Shanks and his crew watched as a hose was brought from the U-boat to the Raleigh. "Fuel," said Crayton. "They're pumping out our fuel."

"And look there," said Billings, the ship's cook. "Those are bins from our larder."

"They're foraging," said Shanks grimly. "They can't put into port, so they're stealing what they need to stay at sea."

Two hours later, the lifeboat had drifted more than a league from the Raleigh, but Shanks and his men could still see the activity between the ship and the submarine. Finally the fuel hoses were withdrawn and the Arges, still on the surface, moved away from the ship.

The U-boat chugged in a lazy circle and halted between the Raleigh and the lifeboat. A series of explosions rocked the ship, echoing across the water. In moments, the Raleigh began to list to port and then to slowly dip into the water like a setting sun. "They've blown her up from the inside," said one of the men.

"Conserving their torpedoes," said Shanks absently as he watched the Raleigh sink beneath the waves.

"Maybe we can rig a sail, sir, once they're gone," said Crayton, "or at least figure some way to signal. Some ship will pass this way before too long."

Shanks said, "I don't think that's what these devils have in mind, Mr. Crayton." In the rosy light of dawn, they could see the Arges resting broadside to their boat at two hundred meters. The leather jacketed crew climbed from the hatches and lined the deck in a rough formation. Koehler stood atop the conning tower as if he were reviewing a parade.

The Raleigh's crew watched as the deck gun was loaded and swung toward them.

Shanks said somberly, "Men, it has been a privilege to be your captain."

"And our privilege to serve under you, sir," said Crayton. "And may the Lord show mercy to us all."

One of the men began to recite the Mariner's Prayer and the others joined in. "Our Lady, Star of the Sea, Mother of God and our Mother, you know all the dangers of soul and body that threaten mariners. Protect your sons and daughters who work and travel on the waters of the world…"

The deck gun boomed and a shell whistled overhead. The gunner was finding the range.

"And protect also their families that await their return. Star of the Sea,

Mother of the Church, give light and strength to those chaplains and lay ministers who bring the love of your Divine Son..."

The gun roared again and the second shell blasted the lifeboat to pieces, scattering men and debris like a handful of straw in the wind. The Arges' crew cheered and applauded.

Crayton bobbed to the surface gasping for breath. He saw a good sized piece of the lifeboat a few meters away but hesitated to swim for it, thinking that riflemen from the U-boat would shoot any survivors they saw, but as he watched in fascinated horror, the men filed into the hatchway and disappeared from the deck. In a moment, the submarine glided away and disappeared beneath the waves, leaving Crayton and his few surviving ship mates in the hands of the sea and Dame Fortune.

Some died at once; some bled out soon after. By nightfall, only Crayton and Billings were left alive, clinging to opposite sides of the lifeboat's splintered prow. Through the night Crayton called to Billings to keep him awake, but finally, near dawn, the cook failed to answer, and Crayton was alone in the middle of the cold Atlantic.

Robbie Crayton woke in a berth on the freighter Glendon out of Liverpool two days after the Raleigh sank and lived long enough to tell his tale to her captain. "I can't say for sure how long I drifted on that piece of wreckage—two days in all you tell me. I woke up here and that's all I remember."

"And the markings on the submarine, and the uniforms," said the captain. "You're certain the ship was German."

Crayton coughed and spat blood into his palm. He stared at it a moment then said, "Aye, sir. She had the iron cross on her tower, but she had other markings as well. The great eye surrounded by thunderbolts. She was the Arges; I'd swear to it on my mother's soul. She sank the Hannity when I was on board, and I'd know that demon boat in the black of night."

"Would you like to take the helm, Commander Cruickshank?" Thomas Wentworth, the American Captain of the luxury liner Galatea stepped away from the ship's wheel. He was ruddy, red-haired, bearded and broad-shouldered. In his uniform Wentworth looked every inch a seaman.

"It would be an honor, Captain." Cruickshank's accent was a notch above Cockney, and two below Oxford. The tall man took Wentworth's place and felt the power of the diesel engines throbbing through the deck and power inherent in the wheel, like Phaeton taking the reins of Zeus's celestial chariot, he thought.

Baines, the wiry little navigator called out, "Course correction two degrees starboard, sir."

Cruickshank eyed the compass and turned the wheel, marveling at the smooth command it provided. The Galatea was as fine a ship as he had ever seen and her operation lived up to her looks. "Two degrees starboard, Mister Baines. Steady as she goes."

"Steady as she goes, Commander."

"Quite a difference between piloting this lady and a sub-chaser, eh, Cruickshank?" said Wentworth with a proud smile.

"She's a fine ship, Captain; no doubt of that."

The Galatea was the star of the Hubley line, a new luxury liner like none before it, outfitted for an elite clientele. More compact than the average ship, her passage was prohibitively expensive for all but the wealthiest. She carried no cargo beyond the needs of the passengers and crew, and she offered no accommodation less than first class; no steerage to defray costs. The ship was extravagant, opulent; an expression of the post-war relief Americans felt, an almost decadent indulgence they believed they deserved for their victory, and a thumb to the nose at the defeated.

The passage from New York City to London was the Galatea's second voyage. On her shakedown cruise, the ship beat the standing trans-Atlantic speed record and Wentworth hoped that this voyage would do that record better. The seas were favorable and barring some unforeseen mechanical problem, the Galatea should arrive in England in two more days, as much as six hours earlier than scheduled.

"You will be joining me for dinner this evening, Commander Cruickshank?" said Wentworth, taking the wheel again.

"It will be my privilege, sir," said Cruickshank. "I should go to my cabin now to dress." The Commander excused himself and as he left the bridge, he looked aft at the setting sun. He wanted to tell Wentworth the risk they were all taking, but he feared that if Wentworth knew, he would feel compelled to take measures to protect the Galatea and its passengers, measures that could not go undetected by inimical eyes.

In his stateroom, Cruickshank closed the porthole and pulled the curtain over it. He looked around the chamber and marveled at the accommodation. It rivaled the best hotels in Paris and New York in its sumptuousness. Mahogany and brass gleamed in the soft lighting, and the bath shone in pristine porcelain white. An ample basket of fruit with a bottle of wine stood on a table near the passage door, compliments of the Hubley Line.

In three days, King George would knight Robert Cruickshank for his valor in the Great War, specifically for his pursuit of the German U-Boats that menaced military and civilian craft alike. Cruickshank locked the bathroom door behind him. He looked into the mirror over the sink and began to methodically remove his face.

In a moment, Secret Agent X regarded his own visage in the mirror. No matter how many times he changed his identity, X always felt a sense of relief to see his own face and be himself again, if only for a few moments. Lesser men might have been driven mad by such total immersion in another's identity, but Agent X had long since become accustomed to it.

American and British intelligence took a particular interest in the disappearance of ships in the North Atlantic beginning in 1919 and began investigating the matter in earnest when a lone survivor of the freighter Raleigh was picked up in the middle of the ocean. The survivor was first mate Robbie Crayton, who died soon after his rescue but lived long enough to tell an incredible tale of a new brand of freebooting to naval investigators.

Only a few days before, Agent X had been summoned to the presence of the mysterious K-9. Their meetings took place in random locations, this time in an empty office in an abandoned warehouse near the New York waterfront. X sat on one side of an opaque screen while his anonymous superior spoke from the other using a mechanical filter to distort his voice, turning it into a steel-wool whisper. "What do you know about U-boats?" he asked.

"What we all knew about them during the war, most of it statistical data. They crippled British and Allied shipping from 1914 to 1918; I believe the tonnage lost was over two million the last year of the war. The Kaiser launched over 350 of them in four years, but the U-boats were a risky business for their crews. Over half of them were sunk. I was taken aboard a captured U-boat once, so I have an idea of their general makeup."

"And is the name Wilhelm Koehler familiar to you?" K-9's voice rasped.

"The U-boat Captain known as the Cyclops. As I recall he was the most successful at sinking our ships, and it earned him a special dispensation from the Reich. Koehler was educated as an engineer before the war and worked at designing U-boats for the Kaiser. He was largely responsible for the refinements of the Type 3 design. Koehler's face was badly burned in an explosion in the shipyard; he lost an eye too, hence the nickname. As the war escalated and more commanders were needed, he was given his own command.

"He designed and oversaw the construction of his own U-boat, a kind of super submarine prototype, a little larger, a little faster, a little more undersea range. It was the only one in their navy that had no number; U-64, U-47, like the others in their fleet. Kaptain Koehler was allowed to name his U-boat Arges after the Cyclops in Greek Myth who personified lightning. The official word has it that a British sub chaser sank the Arges near the close of the war. The depth charges did the job. All hands were lost."

"Unless someone is pursuing a grotesque masquerade, Koehler is alive and well, and so are his ship and crew," said K-9. We have learned that he is apparently sinking ships at random in the North Atlantic."

"Is it piracy? Extortion? Has he made overt demands of any person or government?"

"No," said K-9, his snarl betraying his agitation. No demands; no rhyme nor reason. So far, we and the British have kept this under wraps, but if it gets out, apart from the loss of human life and disruption of commerce, we face an issue of image. The Great War was supposed to be the War to End All Wars. America and the Allies were supposed to make the world safe and stable again, and this terrorist calls to question its confidence in us. He must be stopped and quickly."

"And how can we do that?" said Secret Agent X.

"In the center drawer of the desk at the end of the room is a sheet of paper. Read it and destroy it before you leave here. It will be up to you to carry out this mission. I can only hope that you are successful." On the other side of the screen, a door closed and X realized the meeting was over.

He opened the desk drawer and unfolded the sheet of paper he found inside. As he read the plan, the hairs on the back of his neck rose. The plan was bold, brilliant, but irresponsible because it put the lives of hundreds of unknowing people at risk. It would be up to him to see that that risk was never realized.

Two days later Secret Agent X lay in wait in the darkened hotel suite of Commander Robert Cruickshank, late of the Royal Navy. The press reported that King George intended to knight Cruickshank in a ceremony at Buckingham Palace twelve days hence. Cruickshank distinguished himself during the war by sinking eighteen U-boats, chief among them Wilhelm Koehler's Arges. So celebrated a figure sailing on the flamboyant Galatea should prove an irresistible target to the Cyclops. Terror and vengeance in a single stroke.

X settled into an overstuffed chair to the side of the suite's entrance and laid his revolver across his thigh. The Waldorf Astoria rivaled the finest hotels in Europe and the management provided Cruickshank with the best of the best, as befit so heroic a celebrity. At least Agent X's wait would be a comfortable one.

A few minutes past midnight, he heard a key in the lock. Cruickshank stood in the doorway for a moment saying goodnight to some friends then came into the suite alone, closing the door behind him. The Commander wore tails and carried a top hat and gloves in his hand. An overcoat draped his shoulders and a white silk scarf hung around his neck.

He turned on the lights and as he did, a voice came from behind him. "Good evening, Commander." Cruickshank whirled and stared, not at the revolver pointed at his chest but at the face above the pistol, his own to the last detail.

"What… who are you?"

"My apologies, Commander. From this point forward, I must be you. We all have a role to play." Secret Agent X squeezed a small bulb in his hand and a cloud of grey vapor blew into Cruickshank's face. The gas took hold, Cruickshank's eyes rolled back in his head, and the Commander slumped unconscious to the floor.

And now, the real Commander Cruickshank was confined incommunicado in a cabin on the Jenna, an armed American ship disguised as a freighter, shadowing the Galatea at a distance of thirty miles. X would have preferred a closer tail, but understood that a nearby ship would perhaps deter Koehler from attacking. He pulled his suitcase from beneath his berth. Concealed in the bottom was a compact portable wireless unit. He switched on the power and opened a special frequency. A few taps of the code key and he raised the Jenna, gave an all-clear signal, and after their acknowledgement, he put the wireless set back in its hiding place.

In the bathroom he opened the small travel case on the shelf beside him and beneath its false bottom found his disguise kit. Agent X shaved carefully and reapplied the liquids, plastic compounds and powders that transformed him once again into Robert Cruickshank. The tuxedo was next, and in a few minutes, Commander Robert Cruickshank was on his way to the Galatea's dining room.

The ship's dining room was a miniature of the grand salon of the Hotel Ritz in Paris, recreated in loving detail by a team of designers and craftsmen. Overhead a chandelier of one thousand crystal teardrops cast rainbows about a room resplendent with linen tablecloths, polished silver, and the miracle of fresh cut flowers four days at sea. Outside, the sky had darkened to twilight indigo and the room glowed like an island of light. Most

"My apologies, Commander."

of the passengers were already seated and enjoying the strains of Mozart from a string quartet at the end of the room.

Agent X crossed to the Captain's table and took one of the last two empty chairs. Captain Wentworth, in full dress uniform, was already at table and regaling his guests with the story of a violent storm that nearly sank the Galatea on her maiden cruise.

Secret Agent X had no sooner pulled his chair into the table when the empty chair beside him was pulled away. A waiter held the chair for an elegant young blonde woman in an emerald green gown. She was seated and said her hellos to her table mates, saving X for last. She turned to him and smiled wickedly, "So, I've finally caught up with you." Her blue eyes sparkled with amusement.

Agent X smiled at the young woman. "I wasn't aware you were pursuing me, Miss…"

"Dale, Commander Cruickshank," she said, holding out her hand, "Betty Dale." Her handshake was firm and her eyes told Agent X this was no flirtation; she was all business.

Secret Agent X knew Betty Dale all too well. He had met the winsome young reporter for the *Herald* more than once in the course of his adventures, but she had never seen his true face. Her remark startled him, but he quickly realized that she believed he was Robert Cruickshank. It was testimony to Agent X's artistry in disguise and impersonation that she could sit two feet from him and not know his true identity.

"Pleased to meet you, Miss Dale… it is Miss?"

"Yes, Commander, Miss. And is there a Mrs. Cruickshank?"

"No, not yet," he said with a smile.

"I knew that, of course. It's part of my story."

"Story?"

"I'm a newspaper reporter, and the *Herald* sent me on this cruise specifically to get the scoop on a soon-to-be knight."

The waiters were fussing with the water glasses and the scent of rich food wafted from the galley. "The papers made such a fuss about it the last few days I'd think people would tire of it by now."

"Not my readers. They want to know every detail. I've been trying to pin you down for an interview since we set sail. If I didn't know better, I'd think you were avoiding me."

The truth was that Agent X had been avoiding her for her protection, not wanting her to become enmeshed in his operation as she had a few times in the past. He also was wary that her reporter's nose might sniff out his disguise and compromise his plans. "Not at all, Miss Dale." His gaze swept the table. "I don't see a notebook."

"The dinner table is no place for a candid interview, especially with six other people nearby. I've found that an audience often inhibits frank answers. I thought maybe we could meet to talk just the two of us, later."

"Before we do, tell me, what do you know about me?" said Secret Agent X, cleverly sounding her out to review his knowledge of Cruickshank's life and career and to avoid making contradictory statements.

"Well, Commander," Betty smiled and her eyelids lowered. "You were born in 1878 in Bromley, Kent. Your father was a haberdasher and your mother taught piano lessons in your town. You were educated locally but spent your final year at Cheam where you played fly-half on the rugby team. You entered the Royal Navy in 1896 and rose in rank to Commander early in the war.

"When the threat of German U-Boats loomed large, the British Admiralty commissioned over 500 'sub-chaser' launches to protect the coastal waters. In 1916 you were put in command of PC-184. For the remainder of the war, you and your crew distinguished yourselves by sinking eighteen U-boats. The most notorious of your victories was won against the U-Boat called the Arges, commanded by the legendary Wilhelm Koehler, scourge of Allied military and commercial ships. You left the Navy after the war ended, and have since become an advisor for American shipping companies and the military. And now you're about to be knighted for your service. How am I doing so far?"

"Bravo, Miss Dale." X clapped his hands silently and smiled. "I'm impressed that you recited all of that from memory. You seem to know everything there is to know about me."

"But what I know is what everyone knows," the pert reporter said. "I want to know the real man behind that handsome face."

Agent X stifled a chuckle. "You'd be surprised what's behind this face, Miss Dale." He looked across the room. "The masked ball is this evening. Could we schedule the interview for, shall we say, ten tomorrow morning?" She nodded assent. "But for tonight," he went on, "Let's have no more talk of knighthood, or wars, or ships. Agreed?"

Pouting, Betty nodded. "All right, but you'd better not stand me up tomorrow, Commander," she said with a laugh. "The story I'd write if you stiffed me on the interview would be a lot less flattering. And by the way, you look just as dashing in that tuxedo as you do in your dress whites."

Secret Agent X gazed across the room. "It's just another uniform, Miss Dale, just another uniform. Ah, here's the bisque."

The elegance of the menu rivaled the setting, and X spent the rest of dinner engaged in pleasant banter with Betty Dale and others around the table. If Betty had any inkling of Agent X's identity, she gave no indication. X had helped her family once, and the few times they were thrown together since, it became obvious that she was smitten with him, but he never took advantage of her affection, though he found her very attractive.

The calculated risk of using an ocean liner full of passengers as bait to draw out Koehler disturbed X enough, but having Betty Dale on board raised the ante. He couldn't let her presence distract him from the mission.

After dinner, Secret Agent X stepped out onto the promenade and stood at the railing, smoking one of Cruickshank's trademark cigars. His eyes swept the surface of the moonlit sea, looking for anything amiss and seeing nothing but the silver eye of the moon reflected on the waves.

A white jacketed steward approached. "Sir, may I get you anything?"

"A gin and tonic, thank you," said Agent X although he had every intention of pouring it over the side as soon as the steward walked away. As much as he might enjoy a good stiff drink, he had to keep a clear head. In many ways, the worst part of any mission was not the physical combat, the mortal danger, but the intense edgy anticipation, the need to be hyper-alert to everything around him, waiting for the ball to land in his court.

A voice from behind him said, "He envies you, you know, sir." It was Baines who spoke, taking a place at the rail beside X. "Captain Wentworth, I mean. Most of us were in the Merchant Marine service and never saw any action in the war. I think the Captain wishes he'd been in the thick of it, as I suppose we all do. You never know how much a man you truly are until you've been tested. It must have been a great satisfaction to kill that murderous bastard Koehler."

Agent X studied the end of his cigar. "It's a delicate balance a man maintains, killing under orders. On one hand, you have the sense of relief that you've killed them before they kill you, but if taking life ceases to trouble your conscience, you become less than a man and more of an animal. Yes, I was relieved that Kohler and his ship were destroyed, Mister Baines, but the memory of human bodies, whole and part bobbing to the surface haunts me to this day.

He paused and took a long pull at his cigar. "What was it Milton wrote? 'They also serve who only stand and wait.' Mister Baines, you and your mates stuck your necks out at least as far as the rest of us did. Twice as many American Merchant Marine vessels were sunk as were your combat ships."

"True, Commander, but twice as many fighting sailors died as did our kind."

"You sailed under-armed into hostile seas; a bow gun, an aft gun and a few machine guns aboard against battle cruisers and U-boats. Who's to say what took more courage?"

Baines nodded and was quiet for a moment then said, "But just once, sir, I wish we'd had the chance to show the Krauts what we were made of."

You may still have that chance, thought X, and sooner than you think.

Later that evening the Galatea's ballroom glowed in the light of thousands of candles, creating an almost magical aura as the dancers glided over the polished floor. Diamonds, emeralds and other gems sparkled in the light and so did the eyes of the revelers behind their masks as they basked in the dreamlike atmosphere.

A liveried attendant handed Secret Agent X a scarlet-feathered mask with brows that swooped upward like horns as he entered the ballroom. The string quartet was now joined by brass and woodwinds and music filled the room. Agent X donned the mask, shaking his head at the irony of covering one disguise with another, and crossed the room toward the bar where a knot of people were drinking champagne.

Agent X recognized Betty Dale by her emerald gown and the cascade of her honey-blonde hair. A peacock feather domino complimented the shade of her dress. Her laughter gave X a pang as he thought of the danger in which his mission placed her. She was speaking to a man in a silver mask with a long nose when she saw X in the corner of her eye and stopped in mid-sentence. She turned to him and said, "Good evening, Commander Cruickshank."

Secret Agent X smiled. "I'm afraid my mask isn't much of a disguise, is it, Miss Dale."

"Nor is mine apparently," she said with a laugh.

Captain Wentworth danced past, holding a bejeweled matron at arm's length. He nodded to the couple as he passed. Just doing his duty. "Would you care to dance, Miss Dale?"

"It would be a pleasure, and please call me Betty." She turned to the man in the silver mask and handed him her glass. "Excuse me, Ronald. I'll talk with you later." As they entered the swirl of dancers, Betty said, "Thank you for rescuing me. Ronald has been pestering me ever since we set sail."

"You can't blame a fellow for that," said X. "You're an attractive young woman."

Betty's head turned away and her smile faded. "I'm afraid my heart belongs to someone else," she said wistfully.

"Lucky he."

"Unlucky me." she said and sighed.

The band broke into a fox trot and the pair shifted gears with ease. "You dance quite well, Commander. I'm impressed. I'm learning more about you every minute."

"I try to keep up," he said.

"We move so nicely together, it's as if we've known each other for years."

"Serendipity," X said. "Kismet, perhaps."

"Kismet?"

"A Turkish word for Fate."

Her eyes sought his behind the feathered mask. "Do you believe in Fate, Commander?"

"I believe each of us makes his or her own Fate, Betty."

The song ended and over the applause, the orchestra leader said, "At the end of this song, it will be midnight and time for all to unmask." The orchestra struck up a lively ragtime song. "I'm not sure how to attack this number," said Agent X with a laugh. "Perhaps we should sit this one out."

At that instant a muffled explosion sounded below decks and the Galatea shuddered. The music stopped and after a few startled cries, the room filled with anxious murmuring that rose to a low rumble verging on panic. Memories of the Titanic and of the Lusitania were still fresh in everyone's mind.

All eyes turned to the Captain. He clapped his hands loudly over his head and called for attention. "Ladies and gentlemen, please remain calm and stay where you are. I'm going to the bridge to determine the situation, and I assure you we'll have it in hand shortly. For the moment, please remain here."

He turned to the orchestra leader, and said one terse word: "Play."

The wide-eyed conductor nodded and raised his baton. In a moment, music drowned out the crowd's apprehensive buzz. As he crossed the dance floor, Wentworth took Agent X's elbow and said quietly, "Come along, Cruickshank; you may be of some assistance."

Secret Agent X squeezed Betty Dale's hand. "I must go," he said. Looking into her eyes, he saw uncertainty. He hesitated a moment and with his forefinger drew a tiny X in her palm. Her eyes widened behind her mask for a second then she nodded resignedly.

"You'd better get your notebook, Betty," Agent X said quietly, dropping his British accent. "You may have a bigger story than you ever dreamed." Without another word, he turned and started for the bridge.

He was halfway down the deck when he saw the prow of the U-boat break the surface close at hand like a dagger through a blanket. As the submarine leveled off, Secret Agent X saw in the moonlight, the staring eye ringed with lightning bolts. The Arges had arrived.

As he entered the bridge, a shell from the Arges' deck gun exploded overhead shearing the mast with the wireless antenna. The crowd in the ballroom ignored the Captain's order and poured onto the deck crowding the rails and craning their necks for a look at the intruding vessel. A burst of machine gun fire over their heads sent them scurrying back indoors. A hatch on the conning tower opened and a tall, dark figure emerged. His voice barked with a thick German accent from a megaphone. "Ahoy, Galatea. This is the Arges. Prepare to be boarded. Resisters will be shot."

On the bridge, confusion ensued. X could see the lack of combat experience put the crew of the Galatea at a great disadvantage. "Mister Baines," shouted Wentworth, "Status report!"

"We've lost our rudder and port screw, sir, and we're taking in water. We've had to seal off the aft compartments and can't get in for repairs, even if they could be done. The best we can do is sail in a circle."

"Ready the lifeboats and alert the passengers, Mister Baines," said Wentworth.

"Wait, Captain," said Agent X "With all due respect, don't stop the engines."

"I don't understand, Cruickshank. What do you propose we do?"

Secret Agent X smiled grimly. "Use our only advantage, our bulk."

The Arges turned in a long lazy arc and slowed as it came along the port side of the Galatea. Black clad men scrambled onto the U-boat's deck from the hatches like ants from a nest. She lay only a few meters from the Galatea's hull.

"On my order, Mister Baines, full astern."

Baines's eyes glistened. "Aye, Captain, full astern on your order."

The submarine chugged slowly parallel to the liner as if it were pulling up to a dock. When it was halfway to the ship's bow, its engines dropped to an idle. Wentworth gave the order. "Engines full astern!" Baines pulled the handle to the engine room telegraph, and the power of the ship rumbled like a waking lion. The single screw took hold and the Galatea began to swivel to port, slowly at first but with increasing speed.

It took a moment for the crewmen of the Arges to realize what was happening. From the upper deck, Agent X saw them drop their ropes and gaffs and scurry for the hatches. Koehler disappeared from the conning tower. The Arges' propellers kicked in and the sub began moving, but too late to avoid collision.

Like a graceful ballet, the two ships moved with exaggerated slowness, and when the impact came, it rocked the smaller vessel, bringing the momentum of forty thousand tons to bear. The Arges listed to port. A handful of the submarine's crew fell from the deck and swam desperately to avoid being run over by the turning vessels.

The Arges surged desperately forward, scraping along the Galatea's hull with a hellish screech, as the ocean liner brushed it sideways like a bathtub toy.

Secret Agent X ran to the wireless room. Clegg, the operator sat frozen at his key. "Damn it, man, get out there. They're too close to shoot. Rig some kind of antenna to get a signal off." Startled by the ferocity of the command, the operator leaped from his chair and darted out of the cabin.

The sudden silence when the Arges cleared the bow of the Galatea was almost as unnerving as the shriek of dragging metal. Through the windows of the bridge, Agent X and Wentworth watched the Arges pull away and slowly submerge.

"Your idea worked, Cruickshank, but I hope you have another. I have a feeling they will be back."

"I'm afraid you're right, Captain, and soon."

Secret Agent X left the bridge and hurried to his cabin to send a distress call to the Jenna. Outfitted with guns and depth charges, she could better deal with the Arges. He turned on the power and tapped out the code for the Jenna. The Jenna's wireless operator tapped out acknowledgement. X sent a terse message: Under attack. Come at once.

And he waited. And waited. A moment later, the Jenna came back with a chilling message: Picking up survivors freighter Martha Wayne. Apparent victim of rogue submarine. Will respond as soon as possible.

What a clever fiend, thought Agent X. Koehler attacked the Martha Wayne but instead of killing survivors as he did in previous raids, he left them alive to draw any nearby ship away from the Galatea, preventing interference and leaving him to carry out his plan at his leisure. Koehler was perhaps insane but far from stupid.

They will return, thought X, and boarding us is inevitable. Our only hope is to stall Koehler until the Jenna arrives.

Before returning to the bridge, Agent X ran down the deck to the ballroom where most of the passengers remained. He found Betty Dale standing at the bar writing furiously in a top bound notebook. She had proven herself capable in the past, and now, X would have to rely on her to save the lives of the passengers and crew, and perhaps his own as well.

"We're moving again. What's happening?" she said, her voice urgent. Around them the buzz of the passengers competed with the ongoing music.

Secret Agent X responded quietly. "A U-boat torpedoed us, the Arges."

"The Arges? But how…?"

"I can't explain now. We pulled a stunt that won't work again but it bought us some time. I only hope the collision with the U-boat damaged it enough to hinder its operation. We'll keep steaming in circles at as high a speed as we can to make a harder target, but a ship this size is tough to miss."

He leaned closer to her and said in her ear, "You know Morse code." She nodded. "I have a wireless unit in my stateroom. It's set to a secure frequency to communicate with an armed ship nearby, the Jenna." He handed her his stateroom key. Quickly he told her where the unit was hidden and the code for hailing the shadow ship. "The Jenna should be coming soon, but so will the enemy. Go there now and keep them apprised of what is happening."

"But why…" At that moment a scuffle began at the main entrance archway between Ronald, a stout, red faced man in a tuxedo and a pair of stewards trying to keep him in the ballroom. "You don't understand," he shouted. "I have to go to my stateroom now!"

"It's Cruickshank they want," said Agent X, "and as far as anyone knows, I am he."

An edge crept into Betty's voice. "You were put on this ship. You knew this would happen."

"Intelligence thought it might. It turns out they were right."

"Bait! You were bait! And all these people are in jeopardy. How utterly irresponsible!" Anger flashed in her eyes.

"Yes, but we're here now and we have to deal with the situation. I need your help to save these people."

More passengers entered the fray at the archway and two of the stewards abandoned the exit they were guarding to help. X grabbed Betty's arm and pushed her through the unguarded doorway. In seconds they were on the deck. "Go," he hissed and turned the other direction to return to the bridge. Betty hesitated a moment, watching the retreating figure, then turned and ran for Agent X's stateroom. As she turned the key in the lock, a second explosion shook the ship.

"Bait! You were bait!"

As Secret Agent X entered the bridge, Baines shouted, "We're hit amidships, Captain. The engine room is flooding."

"Get those men out at once, Baines, and seal the hatches."

Clegg, the wireless operator ran in. "Sir, I've sent out an S. O. S. with our position, but so far no response. I don't know how far a signal will carry from that jerry-rigged antenna."

Wentworth nodded grimly. "Good work, Clegg. Keep an ear on it." He turned to agent X and said in a low voice. "We're dead in the water. If we do hail a ship, what do I tell them? "Come to our aid and risk being torpedoed too? Or just tell them to come later and pick up the pieces?"

To starboard the Arges broke the surface sixty meters away. This time as the leather clad crew men clambered through the hatches, no voice called out the Arges' intention. Everyone knew what would happen next.

"No resistance, men," said Wentworth.

"Sir, we've got to fight them," said Baines to the Captain.

"And risk the lives of every innocent passenger? No, Baines, we have no choice but to submit."

"But they'll kill us anyway," said Baines plaintively.

"Perhaps not, Mister Baines," said Agent X. "I believe I'm the one they want, no one else. Perhaps they'll be content to take me and leave the rest in peace. I'll surrender myself to them."

"I can't let you do that, Cruickshank," said Wentworth. "I'm as responsible for your safety as I am the others."

"What choice do you have?"

Below, the black clad reavers fired line guns over the railings and began climbing their ropes onto the ship. Shortly, ladders were dropped over the side and the boarding party was soon on the bridge. The German sailors held Wentworth, Agent X and the crewmen at gun point while a short officer with a blunt hook at the end of his right arm, likely Koehler's First Mate, barked orders to the men waiting outside the cabin.

Secret Agent X understood German as well as he did English. The command was to search the ship, round up the passengers and crew, and kill anyone who resisted. The intruders hurried to their task and the bridge was quiet for a moment. From time to time the sound of scattered gunfire came, followed by silence.

A shadow filled the door to the bridge. A man with half a face strode in wearing the standard U-boat jacket and cap. Koehler was tall, authoritative, a presence, and although he wore no officer's insignia on his cap, from the moment he stepped onto the bridge it was obvious that he was in command. His one eye surveyed the room. He casually walked around the bridge pausing to study one instrument or another. He finally stood before Wentworth and said with his half mouth, "Your ship is a thing of beauty, an *objet d'art*. But I regret that the British drug addict Keats was mistaken when he wrote that a thing of beauty "is a joy forever.""

Wentworth seethed but held his tongue. Koehler went on. "Your clever maneuver did very little damage to the Arges, nothing substantial. I would compliment you on your pluck and ingenuity, but I realize that your imagination is far too limited to concoct such a scheme."

Koehler turned to Agent X. "But you, Commander Cruickshank, are a resourceful and worthy adversary." Koehler stood toe to toe with X and the pair locked eyes. Neither flinched away.

"You've gone to a lot of trouble to see me, Cyclops," said Secret Agent X, "You could have avoided inconveniencing all these people and just called me on the telephone and made an appointment."

Koehler barked a laugh. "As cocky as ever, I see. But who wouldn't be after the success of a lifetime, putting an end to—what did your British press call me—the Devilfish? The Menace of the North Atlantic? And now knighthood. How ironic that your greatest success has turned out to be your greatest failure."

"The day isn't over yet."

Koehler chuckled. "You British; seldom right but always optimistic."

"Kraut bastard!" From the corner of his eye, Agent X saw a flash of movement as Baines charged across the bridge, a knife in his fist. Before Koehler's men could stop him, Baines lunged forward from Koehler's blind side and drove the blade into the thick muscle of the German's shoulder, narrowly missing his neck. Koehler seized Baines by the throat with his left hand and with his right plucked the knife from his shoulder. Koehler lifted the first mate one-handed until his toes dangled.

Koehler's grip tightened as Baines' turned blue. The German cocked his head to see all around Baines's face as if he were studying a piece of sculpture. "Foolish little man," said Koehler. With a quick thrust he drove the blade into Baines's neck just below the hinge of his jaw and began to slowly and methodically saw back and forth with the blade, cutting toward the front of the First Mate's throat.

Wentworth and X both started forward to help Baines but stopped short when Koehler's thugs raised their guns. Hot blood spurted from Baines's neck. His eyes bulged. Koehler looked into his eyes and said, "Any last words? No?" and sawed through his larynx. In a moment, Baines's head hung back over his shoulders like a gaping hatch.

Koehler dropped Baines's body to the floor and flipped the bloody dagger end over, catching it by the tip. He offered the handle to Wentworth. "Perhaps you'd care to try, Captain." He turned to Agent X. Or you, Commander? Ah, but I forgot; you're accustomed to letting depth charges and paravanes do your killing for you. To know that an adversary is truly dead, watch the light leave his eyes, smell his blood, and then you will know for sure. Otherwise he might come back to return your favor."

"Or to allow me to finish the job."

Koehler smiled with the right half of his face. "Or to perhaps let you live; sometimes a fate worse than death. A delicious irony, that." He reached into Secret Agent X's inside pocket and drew out a cigar. "I'll enjoy this, Commander, while I decide your fate and that of the others."

Agent X stared into Koehler's icy blue eye and what stared back at him was consummate madness.

"It's me you want, Koehler, just take me with you and let these other people go."

"How gallant, Commander," Koehler sneered. "But that would let you die a hero in spite of it all."

Koehler's First Mate returned with news that all of the passengers and crew they could find were gathered in the ballroom. "Let us join them, gentlemen. There is much to be done."

In the ballroom the terrified passengers were huddled along with the crew in a mass, kneeling on the hardwood dance floor, hands behind their heads. Some still wore their festive masks. Agent X scanned the room and didn't see Betty Dale. He was relieved and at the same time fearful that she was the victim of one of the gunshots he heard minutes before. From the deck came the sound of breaking wood. Koehler's men were smashing holes in the lifeboats with fire axes.

"They're destroying the lifeboats," said Wentworth.

"All but one," said Koehler, and he strode away to speak to his first mate.

"What's he talking about? Why leave one lifeboat intact?"

"I'm afraid his plans for all of us are only beginning," said X.

Koehler and his mate returned. "Commander, if you would, please come with me." Before Secret Agent X could protest, two of the Arges' crew took him by the elbows and he was marched out of the ballroom. They took him to the lower deck. The U-boat waited below. "Over the side," one of the crewmen said, nudging Agent X in the small of his back with a Luger. Craning his neck over the rail, X saw a narrow rope ladder dangling from the rail to the water.

Secret Agent X had no doubt he could have dispatched these two ruf-fians with ease, but in doing so, he would surely be killed by their mates and any hope for saving the Galatea's passengers and crew would die with him. Better to play along and buy time in the hope that the Jenna would arrive before Koehler sank the liner. X climbed over the railing and began clambering down the narrow rungs.

As soon as his feet touched the foredeck of the Arges, he was taken through a hatch and into the bowels of the submarine. He peered around him in the dim yellow light to take in his surroundings. The cramped companionway would have made a claustrophobic man leap back out of the hatch screaming. Agent X smelled the unmistakable odors of engine oil, ozone and sweat.

His guards pushed him into a small forward storage room. Koehler's men searched him thoroughly but took nothing from him other than his billfold, his pocket watch, his fountain pen (the one that hid a three-inch blade in its barrel) and his cigar lighter. His cigars remained in the inside pocket of his tuxedo jacket. It's trophies they're after, thought Agent X, proof of my capture; cigars are useless on a U-boat.

The door clanged shut, outside the wheel turned, and the bolt slid into place. X was left in total darkness. Carefully he felt his way around the cramped compartment looking for anything that could serve as a weapon or an aid to escape. There were crates of foodstuffs and even a gallon tin of olive oil. If it were glass, Agent X could have broken it and used a shard as a crude knife. Most of the crates were still nailed shut and he'd need a pry bar to open them. Nothing immediately useful seemed to be at hand, so Secret Agent X fell back on his own resources.

He reached into the pocket of his jacket and felt the bands on each of the cigars until he found the special one with the figure of the lion embossed rather than simply printed on it. Two of the three cigars was ordinary; the third concealed enough explosive to damage the U-boat if not sink it. He was sorry that Koehler had not chosen that one to smoke, but it left him a useful weapon. In their haste, the searchers also left his shoes after pulling them off his feet and finding them empty.

He held one of the patent leather pumps in his hand and rapped it hard on the corner of a crate. The heel came loose, and in a moment X had it off. Inside the heel was a small folding knife with more than just the usual clip point blade. It contained a screwdriver, a tiny file, and a small set of lock picks. The other shoe contained a tiny version of the larger makeup kit in his stateroom on the ship.

Next, he held one of the front buttons on his tuxedo jacket by its stem between his thumb and forefinger, and with his other hand, twisted the cloth-covered cap clockwise, and unscrewed it. (The cap was reverse threaded to prevent discovery by turning it the customary direction.) Inside he felt a glass bead the size of a pea. He slipped the bead into his mouth and tucked it between his cheek and gums. In another he found a half dozen waterproofed Lucifers with stubby stems. Agent X hammered the heels back onto his shoes. After a moment's thought, he unscrewed the cap on the tin of olive oil, set the cap loosely over the spout and put the can on the floor near the doorway. Then he settled down on a crate to wait, wondering what was happening above on the Galatea.

In the ballroom, Wentworth and his crew knelt on the hardwood floor with the passengers, held at bay by three black-clad gunmen. Although the whole incident had taken less than an hour, it seemed timeless to Wentworth, fluctuating between an instant and eternity. The crowd maintained a tense silence, broken only by an occasional anxious whisper from one of the men or soft sobbing from one of the terrified women.

Koehler stood at his ease, smoking Cruickshank's cigar and gazing out the salon window into the darkness. He turned to Wentworth and blew out a lazy cloud of smoke. "I cannot enjoy a fine cigar like this on the Arges. One must take one's pleasures when he can, eh, Captain?"

Two of Koehler's men dragged Clegg through the archway and threw him roughly to the floor. He was badly beaten and barely conscious.

"*Herr Kapitan*," the sailor spoke in German, but Wentworth understood every word. "We found this one hiding overhead near the mast trying to send a message."

Koehler looked dispassionately at the battered man and after brief consideration, pulled his Luger from its holster and shot Clegg in the head. Some of the women screamed, and so did some off the men. The boom of the pistol galvanized the crew and they sprang to their feet, ready to fight back, but as one, they looked to the captain.

More of Koehler's men ran into the ballroom at the sound of the shot, machine guns aimed at the crowd in general. "Steady, men," Wentworth said.

"I say we rush 'em." Growled Mickens, a burly stoker from the engine room. "I don't cotton to die like a steer in a slaughter pen."

Koehler's head turned and his eye fixed on Mickens. "I admire your pluck, sailor. And since you're the only one of this sniveling pack of degenerates who has a backbone, I think you deserve a chance." He turned to his men and barked, "Grauber."

A German at least the size of Mickens snapped to attention. *"Jawhol, Herr Kapitan."*

"Kampfen, diesen Mann." And to Mickens with a shrug, "Kill Grauber and you live."

"I'll take that bet." Mickens stripped off his shirt revealing a thick chest and flat stomach. His biceps bulged, and as he flexed them, his tattoos danced.

Grauber pulled off his jacket and his gloves. Under the left one was a steel hook. The German grinned wickedly and as he charged from one side of the room, Mickens rushed at him from the other. The pair collided with a thud like a pile driver. Neither gave an inch; their force was equal.

They grappled on the floor in a bizarre *danse macabre*, but it was anyone's guess which one of them was Death, and which the dying. Grauben was a seasoned warrior, but Mickens was no stranger to fighting men with blades. They grappled furiously, Mickens keeping himself inside the arc of Grauber's hook and punishing the German with short jabs that broke at least one of his ribs.

Grauber swung his hook upward, narrowly missing Mickens' throat. Mickens grabbed Grauber's wrist and twisted the arm down and forward, nearly bending the German in half at the waist. Mickens drove his fist into the base of Grauber's skull with a blow that would have felled an ox. But Grauber was no ox; he staggered backward but didn't fall.

Grauber lowered his head and rushed at the stoker, butting him in the stomach. Mickens wrapped his burly arms around Grauber's waist and rolled backward, sending Grauber spinning across the floor and crashing into the crowd.

Wentworth shot a glance at Koehler and saw he was watching the fight with a look of near boredom, as if he had no concern for its outcome.

Grauber's chest heaved. Mickens' chest was slick with sweat. The pair circled like dogs in a pit. Grauber snarled and rushed at the stoker. They grappled again and this time Mickens got a hand under Grauber's leg and heaved him off his feet.

Grauber crashed to the floor and rolled away, narrowly avoiding a skull-crushing stomp from the stoker's booted foot and slashed at the stoker. The hook sunk home in Mickens' side and the giant bellowed in rage and pain. Grauber twisted the hook and tore a gobbet of flesh from Mickens, but before he could strike with it again, Mickens crashed on top of him, driving his knee into the German's solar plexus.

Grauber flailed with his left arm, but could do no more than rake Mickens' back and shoulder with his hook. Mickens clamped a hand on Grauber's throat and drove his fist again and again into the German's face, splitting his lips and smashing his nose. Grauber's arms flailed for a moment then dropped to the floor and Mickens closed his other hand around his enemy's throat.

"Mickens, that's enough," shouted Wentworth.

"No, Captain." Mickens jerked his head over his shoulder at Koehler. "Himself says kill him, and so I shall."

Everyone else was watching the drama and didn't see Koehler nod to one of his men. The sailor drew a long tapered dagger and stepped up behind Mickens. With an overhand blow, he drove the point downward into the stoker's chest behind his collarbone. Mickens was dead in seconds, the long blade piercing his heart.

The killer and another of Koehler's men hauled Grauber to his feet. "He lives, Kapitan," said one of them.

The crowd was stunned silent. One of the passengers, a dignified, white-haired man spat coldly, "You lying son of a bitch, you said if he killed Grauber you'd let him live."

Koehler shrugged. "He hadn't killed him yet. Besides, I can't afford to lose any more of my men. It is the most delicious torture, is it not, my friend? A lesson from the Inquisition: allow hope to blossom then crush it underfoot." Koehler turned to his first mate. "Kurtz, prepare to disembark." Then to Wentworth, "Come along, Captain; I have a place of honor for you to enjoy what will follow."

Two of the Arges' crew seized Wentworth by his arms. The Captain broke an arm free and smashed a fist into the face of one before the other clubbed him to the dance floor with a blackjack from behind. This time no one offered resistance. In a moment, Wentworth, was hauled to his feet, his hands tied behind him.

Koehler stood before him eye to eye. "I am pleasantly surprised to see you finally show some gumption, Captain Wentworth. It renews my faith in Mankind to see you fight back. If our roles were reversed, however, I would already be dead, for unlike you I would die before I allowed my ship to be boarded at all."

In the storeroom, Secret Agent X heard the throb of the Arges' engines and felt the shudder as the submarine began to move. The door swung open and one of Koehler's crewmen stood, pistol in hand. One of his ship-mates stood behind him in the passageway. *"Kommen sie,"* he growled in a guttural voice and waved his pistol in a gesture for Agent X to follow him. One walked ahead of X and one behind him with a pistol pressed between his shoulder blades.

From other parts of the ship came clanking, rumbling, and the sound of booted feet on steel decking. Whatever Koehler was planning, its execution had begun. Agent X hoped that Betty Dale was able to get a message through to the Jenna and that help would arrive in time. The agent knew that he couldn't count on that help, however and had no choice but to act in the meantime as if it were not coming.

Secret Agent X had been on a captured U-Boat during the war and although the Arges was larger, its layout seemed similar to Type 3 design. From the storage area, the black-clad Germans marched him through the crew quarters, empty now, past tiers of iron bunks on either side of the compartment. Secret Agent X's practiced eye took in every detail, watching for any chink in the ship's armor that could allow him to cripple the sub. In the control room directly under the conning tower, Agent X saw men intent at their tasks, reading gauges, pulling levers, turning control wheels. Commands and acknowledgements were barked in German as Kurtz brought the six hundred horsepower sea beast to heel.

The submariners marched X past the radio room and through a small chart room then stopped at the door of a closed compartment. One of the Germans rapped on the door. *"Herr Kapitan."*

"Eingeben. Enter."

The door opened inward and Secret Agent X was pushed inside. The gunmen waited in the passageway.

Agent X stood in a Spartan version of his stateroom on the Galatea. Koehler sat at ease in a leather armchair, one booted foot resting on the opposite knee. The black leather jacket and cap lay on the bunk. He looked to the guards and said, "You may leave us. Commander Cruickshank is no fool. He has nowhere to go, and even if he were a fool…" Koehler raised a cloth from the table beside his chair revealing a Luger. The guards nodded and closed the door. Agent X heard the clank of an exterior lock.

"Welcome to the Arges, the supreme *unterseeboot,* and to my quarters, Commander. Not as grand as the salon of the Nautilus or perhaps your own, but… "he shrugged and gestured to the table beside him. Would you care for brandy?"

Koehler poured the amber liquor into two snifters and offered both to Secret Agent X. "Your choice, Commander. You have no need to fear drugs or poison. Let us drink like gentlemen, adversaries who recognize each other's prowess. Although you didn't kill me or sink the Arges, you are the only man who ever came close, and for that, I salute you."

Agent X nodded, taking one of the snifters. "Thank you. You mentioned the Nautilus. Is that how you see yourself? As Captain Nemo?"

Koehler smiled that disarming half smile. "I have so little use for the French cowards, fools, degenerates. Jules Verne is the exception. His ideas inspired me to design the Arges years ago, and they have inspired me in my life's mission."

"And what is that? To avenge Germany?"

Koehler's single eye blazed. "Deutschland." He spat the word. "I am ashamed of my country. "Versailles," he hissed. "To be humiliated and yield to the demands of the French, the Americans, the British. In time the Germans will pay as well for their sins of weakness."

"And how do you hope to achieve that end with only one U-boat?"

"Today there is one. Soon there will be others, and like Nemo, we will rule the seas with terror, and the world will bend its knee. The nations are filled with war's living victims; dispossessed, disenfranchised, disaffected men who would gladly serve a strong master."

Keep him talking, thought X. Stall for time. "But we destroyed this ship, or thought we did. We saw debris, bodies floating to the surface."

"You thought you killed me and my ship. But now we are both back from the dead to return the favor. What was it your T. S. Eliot wrote? 'I am Lazarus returned from the dead to tell you all. I shall tell you all'."

Koehler's eye drifted away from Agent X, gazing into the past. "When your depth charge breached our hull, four of my men were killed outright. We shut down the Arges' engines and let the ship sink. We knew you would be waiting above, listening, watching for us to surface. So we pushed broken furniture, uniforms, papers, anything that would float, and the bodies of the dead through the torpedo tubes."

"But you said only four crewmen died. We saw much more."

"You foolish Englishmen ignored the lesson of the animal that gnaws off its leg to escape a trap. Perhaps you noticed that members of my crew are missing hands, feet, limbs, ears. They made the sacrifice, injured or whole, and were amputated to perpetuate the ruse that we were dead. I set the example." Koehler pulled the trouser cuff of his trouser leg across his knee and tugged down his woolen sock, revealing a steel foot.

"We waited and we waited until our air was so foul it was barely breathable, and only then did we chance raising the periscope. You were patient

"Is that how you see yourself? As Captain Nemo?"

but not patient enough, Commander Cruickshank. I saw you sailing away, smug in your assurance that you had scotched the Cyclops. We limped to shore and affected repairs to the hull so that we could sail again. And now here we are, and here you are."

"It seems that I have underestimated you and your crew and your determination. But how have you managed to keep in operation for the last year alone and unaided?"

Koehler smiled again. "One of the few comforts available to a man under the sea is the gift of reading." He waved a hand to a corner of the cabin where bookshelves were packed with books. "I not only read Jules Verne, I read many Americans as well; Mark Twain, Jack London, Frank Norris, and William Tecumseh Sherman. His memoirs inspired me."

"Sherman inspired you?" said Secret Agent X. "How so?"

"I adapted the brilliant tactic of Sherman's March to the Sea: foraging, living off whatever the captured and conquered have to offer and destroying all else. It terrorizes and demoralizes the enemy and motivates one's men to action."

"That will take you only so far, Captain. How long do you think the world will allow you to run free on the ocean before you're hunted down?"

"Hunted down? Where in a hundred six million square kilometers of ocean do they begin to look? We can hide for a day, a month, a year before we strike again, and we can strike anywhere. The world can't arm every ship it sails, nor demand an escort. Our most effective weapon is the uncertainty where we may strike and when. The terror of us will ultimately paralyze the world, and then it will pay dearly for its security."

Koehler took the last swallow of his brandy and stood. "I apologize for the briefness of our visit." He opened the door to the cabin and Secret Agent X saw the guards in the passageway. "It will be first light soon enough and we can all watch our little drama unfold. Come along, Commander."

Between the guards X followed Koehler through the corridor into the map room. One of the crew blocked the entrance for a moment, tugging at a stuck lever. Agent X looked quickly around the room. Koehler said he put in to shore to repair the Arges. He said he could wait weeks, months. To do that, he would need a hideout, some put-in where he and his men could affect repairs and store ordnance. There was little room on board for extra torpedoes.

His eye fell on a map of the North Atlantic mounted on the wall beside him. A small star marked an island off the Cornish coast. X barely had time to memorize the coordinates before he was nudged forward again past the radio room and into the ship's control room.

Kurtz was looking through the periscope. He surrendered it to the Captain who looked for a moment, grunted and motioned to Agent X. "Come look, Commander. I think you'll find the view interesting."

Secret Agent X looked through the scope and saw waves lapping over the bow of the Arges. Dead ahead lay the Galatea. The brightly lit luxury liner glowed like a diamond tiara. Her upper deck was lined with passengers at the railing, men and women. X could not see Betty Dale but prayed that she was somewhere among the crowd now that Koehler's man had left the ship.

"Look closely above the upper deck amidships, Commander. Do you see your friend Captain Wentworth?"

In the moonlight, Agent X saw a figure hanging from the railing over the side of the ship.

"He's chained to the railing facing the Arges so he can look her in the eye and watch his doom and that of his ship. We are waiting for dawn so that he can see the torpedo coming that sinks his floating Xanadu."

"We're not submerged," said Secret Agent X.

"No," Koehler replied. "For years, my eye at the periscope was the only one to witness our triumphs. I believe my men deserve to share that privilege as well. They will stand on deck to watch the *denouement* of this play. Their diligence and devotion entitles them to that reward, to see their efforts come to fruition. Another reason: look to the left, Commander. Tell me what you see."

Agent X turned the periscope and saw bobbing near the Arges' prow the Galatea's last lifeboat.

"Your last ship, Commander Cruickshank, your final command. You'll be lashed to it and after you watch the Galatea sink to the bottom, you'll be set adrift. Distress calls will be made, and help will come, but only you will be left to tell the tale. Let His Majesty tap your shoulders with his sword then. He'll more likely cut off your head with it, the fraud exposed." Koehler said to the guards, "Take him to the storage compartment until we are ready."

The guards led X to the store room and the first stepped past the narrow doorway to allow the second to push the agent into the compartment. Agent X stepped inside and as he did, he kicked over the tin of olive oil and grabbed the guard's gun hand, pulling him onto the now oil-slick decking.

The guard's hands and feet flailed as he fought to keep his balance. X brought his doubled fists across the back of his head in a vicious rabbit punch and the German fell forward into the compartment. His companion came pistol first through the doorway and X threw his shoulder into the steel door, closing it on the gunman's wrist with a sickening crunch of bone. The gun clattered to the floor.

Secret Agent X kicked the Luger away and yanked the man into the compartment by his broken wrist. He grunted in pain, but fortunately for X, didn't cry out and alert others. The German slipped on the oil and fell back against the steel door, slamming it shut. There was no room to maneuver in the close quarters of the storage compartment and Agent X could not avoid the punishing body blows his opponent delivered. X swung his fist at the man's jaw but he ducked and X's blow caught him on the crown of his head.

The German snarled, his hands clawing for the agent's throat. Agent X grabbed handfuls of the man's jacket and pushed against his chest. The German strained forward as X wanted him to and suddenly, instead of pushing, X pulled him forward, off balance on the slippery decking, and drove his forehead into the German's. This second blow combined with the first did the trick.

As his opponent sagged, Secret Agent X felt a blaze of pain. The crewman on the floor had wakened enough to slash his calf with a short knife. X threw the body of the unconscious German onto his mate and grabbed his attacker's knife hand with both of his own. Agent X twisted the hand painfully and the knife fell to the deck. X jackknifed his legs and dropped to the deck in a crouch, his momentum driving his thumb deep into the ganglion of nerves behind the German's jaw, an Oriental fighting trick, and the fight was over.

Secret Agent X stood sweating over the pair of unconscious men. He listened carefully and heard only the pulsing of the engines and distant clatter of machinery. The fight had gone undetected because the door had closed; what seemed at first a hindrance was an unexpected blessing.

He cut strips from his tuxedo coat and bound and gagged his guards. The wound on his calf was superficial and he tied the white silk breast pocket handkerchief from the tuxedo around it to stanch the bleeding. Agent X then took a leather jacket and cap from the larger of the two and donned it as a makeshift disguise. Pulling the hat low on his forehead, he opened the door and slipped into the passageway. He quietly closed the steel door and turned the tumbler wheel, locking it. Ten meters away toward the bow, a sailor stood at the foot of the ladder to the forward hatch. X nodded once and the sailor nodded back. The disguise afforded him opportunity, but Agent X had only minutes to save the Galatea, and he hoped his memory of U-Boats was correct.

In the middle of the deserted crew quarters a square steel plate lay in the floor. Beneath it was a narrow tunnel for electrical wiring that ran aft between the engines. If he was lucky, it would run to the furthest compartment of the Type 3 U-boat, a rear-facing torpedo room.

Secret Agent X raised the lid and crawled backward into the opening. He pushed his body toward the bow until he was completely inside the tunnel then reached up and slid the steel hatch back into place. And not a moment too soon; booted feet thudded overhead through the compartment just seconds later.

The tunnel was a tight fit and X had to force his shoulders through some of the narrower squeezes. A faint glow shone through ventilation grilles ahead, lighting his path to the stern of the submarine. He passed beneath the control room and chart room and crawled between the throbbing engines, grateful that their rumble covered the scraping of his jacket and his shoes on the decking.

At the stern, Agent X found his way blocked by a solid steel panel. The only way out of the tunnel was the plate overhead. X rotated his body and carefully pushed the plate upward with his fingertips and his forehead, looking toward the bow from the bottoms of his eyes. No one was in sight. He rotated again and pushed upward with his shoulders, gently raising the plate from the deck. He jackknifed his legs under him and his head and shoulders had just cleared the opening when the door to the aft torpedo compartment swung inward, showing X a pair of booted feet.

"*Was ist das?*" the sailor said, surprised at Agent X's appearance but fooled by his disguise in the dim light. X sprang up from the tunnel. He bit down on the glass bead in his cheek and as he did, he exhaled sharply, blowing a cloud of knockout gas into the sailor's face. The bearded German's eyes rolled back in his head and he tumbled backward into the compartment.

Secret Agent X heard excited voices from the other end of the submarine. His escape had been discovered. He quickly dragged the unconscious man to the tunnel opening and slid his limp body into it. X replaced the steel plate and ducked into the aft torpedo compartment, closed the door and turned the wheel, bolting it behind him. His eyes searched the room and found what he needed first: a meter-long steel crow bar used to lever the torpedoes into position. He slipped it between the spokes of the wheel and wedged it against the bulkhead, effectively jamming the door.

He was in luck; the single rear-firing tube was empty. A torpedo lay in its rack ready to feed into it. Agent X pulled out the cigar with the special band and bit off its end. He clamped the cigar in his teeth and with both hands grabbed the wheel that manually opened the torpedo tube.

Water gushed into the compartment, forcefully at first, then gradually tapering off as the water level in the room reached the top of the torpedo tube. A heavy pounding sounded through the compartment door. The crewmen were using a sledgehammer. Soon they would break the door from its hinges.

Agent X scratched one of his stubby matches against the hull of the ship and lit the cigar. He took a long pull on it to get it burning hot and wedged it between the torpedo's nose and the rack.

If the tunnel was a tight squeeze, the torpedo tube was even tighter. Agent X thought of the bleeding wound in his calf. Sharks were a risk he'd have to take. He shucked off the leather jacket, took the deepest breath of his life, and shoved his torso into the water-filled tube.

In a minute he was at its mouth and struggling to free his hips. His air was running out. Dark spots swam in his vision. He wiggled his shoulders through, clamped his hands on the rim of the opening, and pushed with all the force he could muster pulling himself free.

Because the Arges idled on the surface, Secret Agent X had only to swim a few strokes before he could take in a lungful of air, but his relief was short-lived. From behind him, a machine gun chattered and bullets tore the face of the water. Agent X gulped air and dove again.

Before he could surface another time, an explosion boomed underwater and the force of it struck him like a giant fist, sending him tumbling end over end. This time when X came up for air, no one fired at him. He swam a good distance before he chanced looking back. Thick black smoke poured from the stern of the Arges. She was crippled now, but still the Galatea was not safe.

Secret Agent X cupped his hands around his mouth, putting them partway into the water. A shaman had taught him years before how to summon animals and to communicate with them. He prayed that he could do the same with creatures of the sea. He whistled the eerie notes again and again.

In the control room, Koehler's eye was fixed to the periscope. The The Arges was listing but the Galatea was still in his sights. "Damn that

Cruickshank. If I be not Nemo, then I be Ahab. 'From Hell's heart I strike at thee,'" he hissed. "Fire the torpedo."

Chained to the side of the ship, Wentworth heard the explosion and saw the smoke and fire rising from the Arges, and soon after, he saw the telltale stream of bubbles coursing toward the Galatea. The torpedo was launched.

Wentworth stared into the eye of the Arges, refusing to turn his face away from death, when a sight to his left caught his attention: a whale spout. A huge blue-grey shape swam on a collision course with the stream of bubbles and pushed against the torpedo's side, turning it away from the Galatea. Doom's instrument sped harmlessly into the cold North Atlantic.

In the control room, Koehler barked into the speaking tube. "Does the rudder answer?"

"*Jawhol*, herr Kapitan."

"Right full rudder. Full speed ahead." Then to himself, "I swear I'll live to cut out Cruickshank's heart."

As the Arges' engines surged, more shapes swam into view. A pod of blue whales surrounded the Arges and pressed against her hull, holding the crippled U-boat immobile. A dozen or more, then twenty, then thirty pressed against the hull of the submarine.

The U-boat's engines strained and the warped screws groaned, but the Arges would not move. In a blind rage Koehler climbed through the forward hatch to the foredeck. He pushed his crew aside, manned the deck gun, and fired point blank into the whales. The Cyclops found himself staring into the large round eyes of the sea and seeing in them vengeful malice. The whales began to pound the Arges, slamming their bodies and slapping their flukes against the steel hull.

Water poured through the hatch as Koehler clambered down the ladder and closed it behind him. "Dive!" he shouted to his crew. Get us away from those damned whales. The Arges slowly sank, as more whales appeared, it seemed, from every corner of the sea.

As the Arges dove, the whales dove with it, pushing the submarine far deeper than Koehler intended until the steel of the hull began to groan where Cruickshank's depth charges had ruptured it once before. And the whales drove it deeper. Koehler staggered to his quarters, ignoring the panicked cries of his crew. He shut the door of his compartment and poured a snifter of brandy.

Koehler held it high and said, "*Morituri te salutant.* Those who are about to die salute you." Before he could finish his brandy, the dark sea crashed through the door.

Secret Agent X bobbed on the surface and saw, near at hand, the Galatea's last lifeboat, broken free from the Arges when the whales attacked. The water was brutally cold, and the lifeboat was his only chance for survival. He swam to it, dragged himself over the side, and collapsed over its gunwale exhausted. He awoke to the sound of heavy engines and the pale light of dawn. The Jenna had arrived. To Agent X's good fortune, the lifeboat lay between the armed ship and the Galatea.

A line was thrown and X was hoisted aboard by eager hands. "Code Devilfish," he said quietly to the crewman who pulled him over the railing. "Take me to Captain Smalley immediately."

Smalley was on the bridge when Agent X approached. "We saw the U-boat dive. We're at the ready with depth charges."

Secret Agent X shook his head. "You'll only harm the whales. The Arges is finished."

"You're certain? And Koehler?"

Agent X stared through the glass at the waves, crimson in the rising sun. "The bottom of the sea is cruel." After a moment's pause, he said, "Please have your men take me to Cruickshank. There's a lot I have to tell him before we reach the Galatea."

An ensign led X to a cabin on the port side of the Jenna. He produced a key and unlocked the door. Inside, agent X saw Cruickshank dressed in seaman's garb and standing at the porthole looking toward the Galatea. Cruickshank turned and the ensign saw both of their faces at once. He looked at X and then at Cruickshank and then at X again in startled confusion. Before he could ask the obvious question Secret Agent X took him firmly by the shoulders and turned him toward the door. "Thank you, ensign; that will be all." He closed the door and turned to Cruickshank. "I have quite a story to tell you, Commander. And you'd best listen to every word."

For the next half hour Agent X related the details of the return of Koehler and the Arges, the plan to draw him out, the seizure of the Galatea, his adventures on the U-boat and its final *denouement* at the hands of the whales.

"And now, Commander, my part in this plot is ended and yours is about to begin. It's time for you to be yourself again. Put on the clothes I'm wearing and Captain Smalley will take you to the Jenna where you can rejoin the passengers and crew. You'll be a hero ten times over after this. If you were American you could probably run for president."

Cruickshank quickly changed clothes with Secret Agent X. "You'll need a new tuxedo, I'm afraid," said X, "but it's a small price to rid the world of a maniac like Koehler and make the seas safe again."

Cruickshank looked away, a flush creeping to his cheeks from his collar. "Being mistaken before about sinking the Arges is bad enough, but now I feel like a real impostor, taking the credit for your heroism. You should be knighted, not I."

Agent X shrugged and turned his palms upward in a gesture of self-deprecation. "I? Knighted? I wouldn't know how to behave. Something else..." X wiped grease from his face with his hands then rubbed it onto Cruickshank's cheeks. "One last detail..." Agent X swung his right fist and caught Cruickshank on his left cheekbone.

Cruickshank staggered backward and almost fell over a chair. "Why, you," he raised his fists and charged at the agent, but X deftly spun aside and with a move honed by countless hours of practice, caught both of Cruickshank's arms and pinned them at his sides. "Easy now, Commander. We can't have a conquering hero come back from battle looking fresh as a new baked loaf of bread." A bruise was already turning purple on Cruickshank's cheek. "Now you look as if you've been in the thick of it."

Secret Agent X let go of Cruickshank who turned to face him. Agent X held out his hand. "Congratulations, Commander, you're about to become more famous than ever."

Cruickshank hesitated for a moment then held out his own and too X's in a hardy grip. He said, "Have you ever read Conrad?"

"*The Secret Sharer*? Very apropos, Commander, for now you and I share a very great secret indeed." X turned as he walked through the doorway into the passage. "By the way, there is a young woman on board the Galatea, a newspaper reporter named Betty Dale. We owe her a story. Tell it to her well."

As the Jenna approached the Galatea, Secret Agent X scanned the crowd of passengers at the railing anxiously looking for Betty. Then he saw her writing furiously, her notebook propped on the top railing. Agent X lowered the binoculars and let out the breath he'd unconsciously held. By the time the Jenna pulled aside the Galatea and Commander

Robert Cruickshank stepped aboard to a hero's welcome, X had removed Cruickshank's face and collapsed exhausted onto a bunk in his cabin. In moments he was sound asleep.

In three days, the Jenna steamed to port in London carrying the rescued passengers and crew of the Galatea. She was met by a barrage of newspaper reporters waiting to interview the hero Commander Robert Cruickshank, soon to be Sir Robert. He left the gangplank and crossed the dock toward a waiting limousine with the noisy entourage shouting questions close behind him.

Only one reporter hung back and stood alone as she watched the pack chase the hero and the story. Betty Dale turned back to the sea to hide the tears that were welling in her eyes. She knew as soon as the Commander spoke to her that he was the real Robert Cruickshank, substituted for Agent X in his disguise. They had all seen the Arges sink. Was Secret Agent X still alive? She knew that she couldn't ask and that Cruickshank couldn't answer even if he knew.

"Excuse me, Miss." A voice behind her. Betty turned to see an older sailor with a seamed, weathered face and bushy white brows. He wore the same uniform as the sailors on the Jenna had worn, but she didn't recall seeing him earlier on the voyage. "I believe you dropped this." He held out a notebook that she recognized as one of hers.

"Thank you, sir," she said reaching out her hand, and as the sailor handed it to her, his rough finger traced a tiny X on the back of her hand. Betty's mouth opened in surprise and the old sailor smiled and put a finger to his lips. "Write the story Betty, the way it must be written." Then he turned and melted into the crowd of passengers and greeters. Tears filled Betty's eyes again, but this time with relief.

Secret Agent X threaded his way through the crowd to the street to hail a cab. He was in a rush to get to the Service's London safe house. He had to get a cable off to K-9. The Arges was gone and Koehler was dead, but there was still the matter of a certain island off the Cornish coast.

THE END

THE SPY GUY

It's always a challenge to write a story using someone else's character(s). As an author, I want to deliver the best story I can and try to be true to the original creator's boundaries and intent. The bulk of Secret Agent X's adventures occur in urban locations and involve cops and gangsters with a touch of mad scientist thrown into the mix. For "Devil in the Deep Blue Sea" I decided to construct a story set immediately after World War I in which X takes on a plausible enemy on behalf of the Secret Service.

There are several themes woven into the story: national interest trumping the safety of individuals, particularly innocent civilians; the concern over maintaining national image as a political tool; personal concerns versus duty; and the unrewarded hero. For my villain, I styled Koehler as brilliant but deluded, seeing himself as a Captain Nemo figure when in the end he sees himself instead as Ahab, pursuing a goal to his own destruction.

I had fun with the U-Boat, basing the Arges on a standard Type 3 design but making it an expanded prototype which is explained in the story. This gave me latitude to play with the sub's size, speed, and other capabilities. So, a super submarine goes after a super luxury liner with many unexpected outcomes.

No Agent X story seems complete without Betty Dale, and I made sure she was on the Galatea and available to help X beat the bad guys. Having her aboard raised the ante for X and added a layer of narrative tension. I try to write things I'd enjoy reading myself, and I hope "Devil in the Deep Blue Sea" hits the mark for all of our readers.

FRED ADAMS - is a western Pennsylvania native who has enjoyed a lifelong love affair with horror, fantasy, and science fiction literature and films. He holds a Ph.D. in American Literature from Duquesne University and recently retired from teaching writing and literature in the English Department of Penn State University.

He has published over 50 short stories in amateur, and professional magazines as well as hundreds of news features as a staff writer and sportswriter for the now Pittsburgh Tribune-Review. In the 1970s Fred published the fanzine *Spoor* and its companion *The Spoor Anthology*. His novels *Hitwolf, The Adventures of C.O. Jones, Six Gun Terrors* and *Six Gun Terrors, Vol. 2, Dead Man's Melody* have been published by Airship 27 Productions.

SECRET AGENT "X"

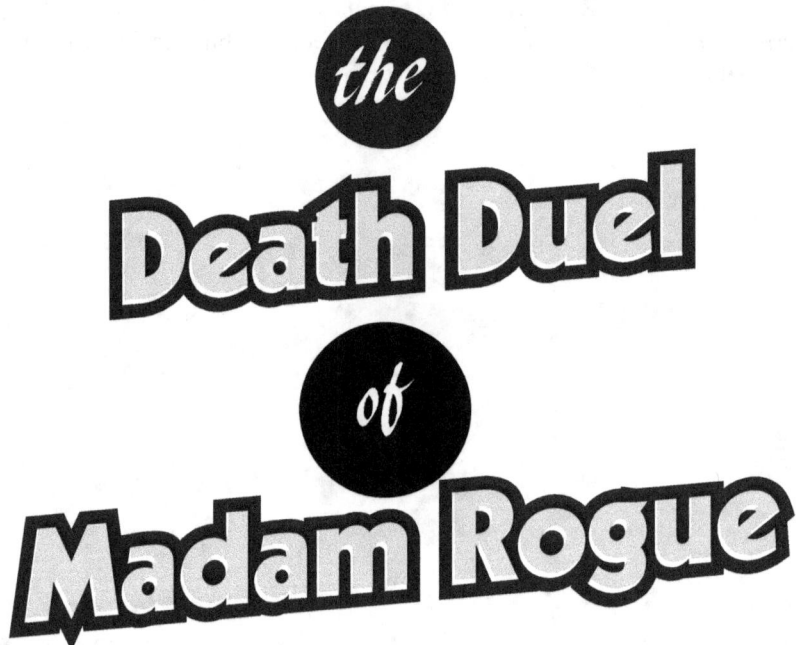

the Death Duel of Madam Rogue

by Frank Schildiner

Edward Stafford was a happy, content man. Why wouldn't he be? He had a large home, chairmanship of one of the largest merchant banks in the United States and a foundation where he was able to help the poor through the tough times. At least three times per week he and his team of dynamic men and women would go out into the worst parts of town and find way to help the unfortunate victims of poverty. Whether it was through food, rent money, better jobs, Edward Stafford and the Stafford Foundation would assist people and ask for nothing in return.

Pouring himself a large glass of buttermilk, Stafford smiled as he thought of the looks of joy on the faces of the families they helped today. The first man had been a pipe fitter, out-of-work for months and about to lose his apartment. The janitorial job in the bank was far better pay than the pipe fitting position, but also enabled the poor man to get a larger home for his growing family. That alone would have been enough, but they'd also rescued a soup kitchen from being closed and supplied all new books for a struggling school. A very, very good day for the Foundation.

Waddling into his study, Stafford sighed again with contentment. His work with the poor had another huge benefit. It allowed him to enjoy another fruit of his family's labor, Faberge Eggs. He loved the jeweled sculpture, knowing they were created for the decadent Romanov Royal Family, but desiring the wonderful pieces nonetheless. The product of the genius of Peter Carl Faberge and his artisans, each jeweled egg was a rare work of art. Only fifty-two were created before the Russian Revolution and Edward Stafford owned five. He'd bought the first from a Russian Prince whose fortunes dwindled thanks to bad cards and unsuccessful marriages. That egg, the Napoleonic Egg of 1912 was a gold masterpiece, crafted from yellow gold and decked with emeralds, rubies and diamonds. The interior contained six tiny panels of beautiful artwork held in place by satin and velvet.

Never one for art before he purchased the egg, Edward Stafford found himself delighted every time he viewed the lovely work of art. Desiring to own more, but feeling guilt for his greed, he'd come up with the idea of the Stafford Foundation to assuage his conscience. Happily three more came into his possession, the Cherub with Chariot Egg, the Necessaire Egg and the Trans-Siberian Railway Egg. The Trans-Siberian Egg was his favorite, containing a gold and platinum train within. When the train was wound up, with a gold key, it was a clockwork toy train with a diamond headlight. A true work of art that made Edward Stafford feel childish delight.

Sipping his buttermilk, Stafford sat down in his favorite leather club chair and picked up the book he was reading, Charles Dickens' THE PICKWICK PAPERS. Owning bound copies of all of the great writer's works, he was determined to read every book the man wrote. Then he thought he would try either Tennyson or Coleridge, remembering some mention of their writings when he was in Harvard studying law. Though avoiding such pursuits in his younger days, Stafford was making up for lost time and learning to love the joy that well-written fiction could bring to the human spirit.

An odd scent entered the air and Stafford sniffed experimentally. It was a sweet, sickly smell, like sugar mixed with something else, pleasurable at first scent, then cloying. He wondered what could cause such a smell, his cook was away for the night and his wife was visiting their grandchildren in London. Perhaps a window was open and one of his neighbors was cooking some odd dessert.

Putting down his book, he made to rise, but found his arms and legs did not have the strength to rise. Alarmed, Stafford struggled to get up again, finding his body weakening with each second. Was this some type of apoplexy? He opened his mouth to call out, knowing a few of the servants were still in their wing and may hear his cries. But only a soft wheeze emerged and he collapsed back in his chair, frozen in place.

A moment later a soft footfall sounded, approaching him from behind. A woman, dressed all in black with a dark hood over her head, appeared. The woman in black stopped before Stafford, bowed in an ironic way and walked over to the Faberge Eggs. With a soft sound of delight, her black gloved hand picked up an egg and turned it in the light.

"Two lost eggs, how nice. And three perfect representations of House Faberge's genius. You are to be commended, sir." The woman in black possessed a soft, flat voice that contained no trace of life. She may as well be a phonograph record; the words were spoken in an odd robotic manner that belied the joy of discovery.

Stafford wheezed again, wishing to demand why the woman would attack him and take his lovely eggs. But once again, no sound emerged.

The woman in black turned and shook her head once, speaking again in that terrible, inhuman manner, "Do not struggle. The Devil Datura plant, when properly prepared, produces a state of near death for those who inhale its vapors. The average time one is frozen is twelve hours, but you need not worry about that."

Once again the woman in black bowed in a mocking manner and walked away. Stafford exhaled loudly, grateful he was going to survive this terrible encounter. The loss of the eggs was horrible, but Lloyds would either find them or pay insurance. And he would look for more eggs, there were others in the world and Stafford was willing to pay.

Just them he felt a slight tickling sensation on his left leg, one that vanished a moment later. Stafford felt it again, this time on his right leg, then both. The feeling was off, a movement that vanished almost immediately and appearing over and over again. He hoped this was merely a reaction from the poison used to freeze him in place.

But then the sensation transformed to a horrific stinging bite, one that caused him to shriek in his own mind but merely cough softly. Stafford glanced down at his leg, his eyes just catching sight of the horrors as they emerged from beneath his dressing gown.

Centipedes, dozens of them crawled on his body, their legs and sharp pincers slowly tearing into his body. He tried to scream, but could not and the pain kept growing…

The headlines of all three morning newspapers were not the planned articles of the tensions on the German and Austrian border, nor the new Mayor's forming a new committee to wipe out the rising gangs in the city. No, they were all changed, without the permission of editors, publishers or even the head pressmen. All three received enormous numbers of complaints for the picture and article that headlined their papers, but sales were huge that day.

The reason for the many complaints was the picture that covered the majority of the front page. The image of a torn and bloody Edward Stafford, covered in ravenous centipedes, was a horrific image that caused many strong stomached adults to become ill. The picture was stark and terrible and many men, women and children wondered if the unfortunate man was still alive when the photograph was taken and developed.

The article was more puzzling to many and even the police, who had some idea of the details. The headline merely read, "A CHALLENGE TO X", in bold type. Beneath the terrible picture the following words appeared:

"You thought me dead, but I live. I challenge you, stop me if you can. Each day I shall murder another and profit from the death. You are the Adam of my labors, but I shall destroy you this time. You have until noon today to save my next victim."

When questioned by the police. All three newspaper publishers and their editors expressed open shock and disgust. But with sales so high, they did not stop the morning presses, but several apologies were planned for the afternoon editions.

Secret Agent X lifted one of the centipedes with a set of tongs, his hands covered by thick rubber gloves. He'd heard of the incident, like everyone had, through the morning papers and rushed to the scene of the crime. His disguise was a simple one Deputy Coroner Alex Jones, a closed-mouthed elderly man who gave sharp answers to any questions. Jones was a perfect guise to use on high profile cases, when X needed to get in and examine the scene without being noticed.

"What is it?" Police Commissioner Charlie Foster asked. Foster was a large graying man who was sharper than he behaved, a good man. X, at times, disguised himself as Foster, especially when he needed to get into the well-guarded police records. But today the idea of pretending to be Foster was ludicrous. X knew the man would be present on such a high-profile murder.

"A bug!" Agent X snapped in his creaky, Jones voice. He saw the slight smiles on Foster's and the nearby detectives and police officer's faces. They knew about Jones's grumpiness and found the behavior an amusing quirk.

"I was hoping for something more specific," Foster rumbled, stifling a chuckle.

X, as Jones, ignored the Police Commissioner for several minutes and finally rasped, "This is a centipede, from Mauritius Island specifically. They're poisonous, but their bite is rarely fatal. However I counted over one hundred bites, which is enough toxin to kill a grown man in a short time."

"Where's this Mauritius?" Inspector John Burks asked. He was a tall man with snow white hair, dark eyebrows and a thin face that was always twisted into a look of stern disapproval. "Down South somewhere?"

"In a sense, yes." Secret Agent X stated, placing the squirming insect into a glass container with the others the police captured. "Mauritius is approximately 1000 miles off the southeast coast of Africa."

"X! This has to be the work of Secret Agent X!" Burks bellowed, slapping a fist into his hand. "Only that fiend would kill a good man in such a horrible way."

"Stop being an idiot," Foster said with a head shake. "Whoever did this, wrote to the papers that he's challenging X."

Inspector Burk shook his head, "Maybe yes, maybe no. This still is X's fault. Because of him a man, who's the closest thing to a saint, is dead. If not for X, the one who killed poor Mister Stafford, wouldn't be here!"

"This isn't helping, Inspector. Find out who the next victim is, fast. We can't risk losing anyone else. That'd send the city into a panic." Foster replied, not noticing as Agent X left the scene in a shaky walk.

The words of Burks stung, because they were all too true. Only one woman, a monster he thought he destroyed years before, would kill in such a horrific manner. A devil who was once the terror of Europe and the United States. A creature who many, Secret Agent X included, believed they'd destroyed in the past, but who kept returning. Her name was almost forgotten but her deeds still were spoken of in hushed whispers, urban legends to many around the world. An expert of disguise and horrifying death. The fiendish master of terror only known to the world as Madam Rogue!

You've returned, old monster. But this time, I'll catch you and make certain you pay for your crimes! Agent X thought as he climbed into Jones's battered, old roadster and drove off. *But who is your next victim? You gave me a clue. You always do, your vanity won't allow you to hide your next move. The answer is in the newspaper article!*

Realizing he needed help, X, still in his Jones disguise, pulled over at a drug store and headed straight for the telephone booth in the back. Closing the cubicle door, he dropped a nickel and dialed a number he knew by heart, that of his most reliable aide, the lovely and brave, Betty Dale!

Betty Dale was fuming as she walked back to her desk, having just gotten into a huge argument with her editor. She wanted to be on the Stafford case, knowing it involved Secret Agent X. She worked with the mystery man and loved him despite his refusal to allow emotions in his life. A true cipher, a mystery even to her, possibly the one person who knew his true face.

But the editor, a self-important fool who felt strange when he had to say his best reporter was a woman, assigned Richmond who was on the crime beat to the case. To him this was just a strange crime, nothing special. This ignored that the murderer seemed able to change the headlines of the town's three papers and murder a prominent citizen in a bizarre, terrifying manner. To Editor and Chief Phil Pulver, the case should be ignored and Betty should stick to working on the next charity function by the local Daughters of the American Revolution or similar groups.

Betty Dale dropped into her chair and ignored the smirk on Richmond's face as she examined the front page again. A beautiful lithe woman with golden blonde hair and large green eyes, she was the amorous interest of many a reporter, police officer or politician when she was out on the job. But she rejected them all, causing them to come to the conclusion that her only life was writing award-winning stories. Those holding that theory could not be more wrong, her true love was helping Secret Agent X save the world. She loved the man and his mission and feared one day one or both may be lost.

Circling a set of words on the headline, Betty heard her phone ring and picked it up, "Betty Dale, how may I help you?" she asked, trying to sound relaxed. She really wanted to hurl the receiver in Richmond's face.

"You know who this is," X stated, his voice still that of Jones. "We spoke two nights ago in the coffee shop near your apartment."

Betty was always amazed by Agent X, never more so than when he spoke to her and sounded like a different person. Today he sounded like a tetchy old man, a voice that could not be further from the true Secret Agent X. But he always, wisely, used identifiers that allowed her to know his identity.

"Yes," Betty replied, sounding as if she was talking about the weather. "I hoped you would call. Do you know who killed poor Mister Stafford? And why? He was a gentle, decent man who used his money to help people."

"Yes to both questions. Stafford was murdered by the fiend known as Madam Rogue. The reason was Edward Stafford owned Faberge Eggs. Madam Rogue loves to steal rare objects of beauty. As to the death, she loves unique murder. She's a monster." X answered, trying to keep himself under control.

"Madam Rogue? I thought she was just a myth. Like the giant who created the Bowery Boys gang. Something to frighten people, penny dreadful stuff." Betty stated, sounding skeptical.

"She's very real. I was forced to work with her in the Great War, until she tried to betray the Allies to the Prussians. I thought she was dead; that I had killed her." X said, his voice sounding both angry and confused. This was his past coming back to haunt him and he never liked to dwell on days long gone.

Betty heard the traces of emotions in Agent X's voice and realized this was the worst direction this man could take. If the Man of a Thousand Faces, the Scourge of Evil-Doers, the Hidden Hand of Justice, allowed himself doubts, the monster from his past would destroy many more lives. No, they needed a strong, confident Secret Agent X now so she didn't ask any further questions about the history of Madam Rogue. That information could come if and when she was defeated.

Instead she took a very different track, "Oh good. You know her methods, so you're the only man she fears. No wonder she's trying to challenge you. Madam Rogue is afraid, terrified of her most dangerous enemy. How can I help?" Betty asked, smiling and sounding happy.

X found himself smiling, realizing his top aide was exactly right. He was about to start dwelling on the days in which he worked with the terrible criminal for Allied Intelligence and their battles once the woman turned traitor. But what did that matter? Agent X knew he was far different than the skilled, but still young man he'd been in the Great War. His training since that time transformed him into someone very different from the pupil he'd been to Madam Rogue. He was now a master agent, a dangerous warrior against the darkness and nothing would change those facts.

"Madam Rogue loves to hint and tease, prove she's smarter than everyone. There will be a clue in the newspaper as to her next crime. I need you to examine every line and every inch of the photograph. I can send you..." X explained, but was cut off by a bark of laughter from Betty.

"The clue, oh that's easy. It's in the article. I spotted it immediately." Betty said, trying to contain her excitement. "I'm guessing you were not an English major in college."

"No, I wasn't." X answered, sounding confused. He didn't want to tell Betty that he only attended universities when he needed to study a particular area like engineering. X realized that his course of study did appear to have some holes, but fortunately he had aides capable of lending their skills to those gaps in his knowledge.

Betty sighed with contentment, knowing she was one of the few that immediately recognized Madam Rogue's riddle. "The article described you as, 'the Adam of my labors'. That's a line from Mary Shelley's famous book, FRANKENSTEIN OR THE MODERN PROMETHEUS. She wrote it in the early 1800's and the book is still famous around the world. There was even that frightening film with Boris Karloff as the monster."

Secret Agent X absorbed the information and then shook his head, "That doesn't help. I mean there's nobody in the city I know of sewing together body parts to create a giant monster."

"Don't be so literal!" Betty snapped, annoyed that X was like her editors in this respect. "The whole book is a metaphor, not a lesson on how to make monsters."

"Explain!" Agent X commanded, grateful he had called her.

"The book was written by Mary Shelley as part of a game. She, her future husband Percy, Dr. John Polidori and Lord Byron were staying in a villa near Lake Geneva and the weather was terrible. Byron proposed a game in which everyone wrote ghost stories. I don't remember what Byron and Percy Shelley created, but Polidori wrote a vampire tale that is still very popular. Mary Shelley created a monster based on the crippled, mad, but brilliant Lord Byron. The creature was poetic, sad and misshapen, taken as a monster by the minds of others." Betty instructed, remembering the lectures from when she was in school all too well.

"Interesting," X replied, still sounding lost. "But that brings us no closer to the next victim."

Betty frowned and leaned back in her chair, "I think if we look at collectors of English literature, possibly we'll find who she's targeting. You said Madam Rogue loves to steal objects of art, correct."

"Yes," Agent X stated and snapped his fingers, "Doesn't the new mayor have a collection of books?"

"Yes, yes he does!" Betty almost yelled and pulled out a file from her desk. It contained information on the mayor, including an article by a rival paper. This was a fluff piece that showed how the wealthy man, who was then a candidate for mayor, was devoting his time to public service. The picture in the article had the man showing the prize of his collection, a Shakespeare first folio.

"Call the Mayor's office now," Secret Agent X ordered, "I'll get over there as soon as possible!"

He disconnected without another word and Betty dialed the operator. She provided the direct number for the Mayor, she being one of the few who knew the private line.

"I'm sorry, that line appears to be engaged," The operator said, sounding bored. "Shall I try again?"

"Yes!" Betty almost yelled, "Keep trying and call me back when you get through!"

She frowned and stood up, grabbing a nearby phone on an unused desk. Betty Dale wasn't going to sit and wait, she would call for additional help. That of Police Commissioner Charlie Foster!

Mayor Calvin Rutherford was also a content man, but not for the same reasons as Edward Stafford. Calvin Rutherford was content because his

"...call me back when you get through!"

world was on the spiral he decided it should be on when he was a young prep school boy, not as wealthy as some, but smarter and quicker than all. Most of his classmates had dreams of lives of ease and luxury, Calvin Rutherford found that to be shallow and dull. He dreamed of power and position.

Which was why at age thirteen, he mapped out his whole life in basic steps. First he would earn a law degree at an Ivy League school, followed by a marriage to a prominent but dull woman of his class. Those parts were simple enough, his grades and athletic record earned him a place at Brown and Martha Winstom's admiration. Winstom's family was old—old money—and possessed the prim and proper attitudes of Puritan preachers. They'd had three children, two girls and a boy living companionable, if distant lives since that time.

But her money and family background made earning a post on several boards quite easy. Then, when the old Mayor was charged with bribery, Rutherford was able to run for the post and win with a huge majority. Another step on his mental checklist achieved. Next he would run for either United States Senator or Governor, whichever looked more winnable. Then it would be a short step towards running for President of the United States or accepting a post like Chief Justice of the Supreme Court. Either way, Calvin Rutherford knew he would be one of the most important men in the world, a historical figure others would study for years to come. That was the plan and twenty five years later, it appeared to be coming true.

The latest incident, the murder of Stafford, could be used as a means of getting there faster. If the criminal was caught quickly, Calvin Rutherford knew he could take credit for the fast arrest. If the killer acted again, he could use this as a means of clearing out all the previous administration's people and blame them continually for the failures. Either way, he couldn't lose.

Returning to his office, Calvin Rutherford greeted his secretary with a perfunctory nod and immediately began preparing a speech he planned on making that night at a banquet. The current incident needed to be added, used as a means of gaining more support for his future political ambitions. Those present would be fearful of receiving the same horrific death as Edward Stafford and they would sign big checks to the man who was promising to not only catch the killer, but would represent their interest all the way to the White House.

Feeling a quick prick of pain under his ear, Calvin Rutherford slapped what he imagined was a fly or mosquito away and continued to write. A moment later his hand fell limp and he collapsed forward on the desk. He was still awake, aware of his surroundings, but unable to move or make a sound.

A strong hand lifted his head, leaning him back so his eyes could see the room. A tall woman dressed all in black with a hood over her head stood before him, looking down at Calvin Rutherford with cold, dark eyes. A moment later the woman turned away, heading straight for the book collection. She removed the Shakespeare first folio and several other items, placing them in a case and bowing in open mockery at the frozen politician.

The woman in black approached Calvin Rutherford again, tossing a silken cord over the nearby chandelier and positioning the rope above the frozen mayor's head. She then tied the rope to the office door and returned to Calvin Rutherford's side, bowing again. Pulling out a large black bag, the woman in black opened the top slightly and poured a small drop of liquid onto the wooden desktop in front of her victim. The liquid hit the desk with a low hiss and a small puff of smoke, a hole slowly being eaten away into the wood.

Calvin Rutherford recognized the liquid instantly, some form of acid. He remembered in prep school chemistry, the teacher dropped a rod of metal into a beaker of sulphuric acid and they'd watched with amazement as the object was eaten away, liquefied in mere seconds. The lesson was both fun and terrifying for everyone, Calvin included, and that stayed in his memory.

The woman in black then tied the bag above Calvin Rutherford's head and produced, with a flourish, a long thin needle. She bowed again and poked a tiny hole in the bag, causing a small drop of the acid to fall on the mayor's head. Calvin Rutherford attempted to scream, but no sounds emerged. The woman in black bowed a third time and vanished from sight, leaving the frozen politician to his agony.

Fifteen minutes later, Moira Taylor, the Mayor's secretary, knocked softly on the door. An elderly spinster in her late fifties, she was a woman who viewed her job as the most important part of her life. Family, pets, outside interests, all were unimportant compared to helping a man like Calvin Rutherford work for the good of all citizens. She knew she was a trusted aide, keeper of the Mayor's schedule and as loyal as a guard dog. Her main job was preventing unwanted visitors such as reporters and rival politicians from interrupting his work.

But it was also her job to remind him of appointments, so when the Mayor failed to respond she opened the door and heard an odd splashing sound as she stepped inside. What she saw caused her to shriek in horror, vomit in disgust and faint dead away. She was kept under doctor's supervision for several weeks after that day. Moira Taylor was rather shaky for the rest of her life, jumping at loud noises and rather resembling a terrified rabbit. She retired to a rest home a short time later, a terrified shell of a woman.

As for Calvin Rutherford, very little of the man was left by the time Secret Agent X and the police arrived at the scene. The torturous acid had nearly killed him by the time Moira Taylor opened the door. But her opening the door caused the bag of acid to crash down upon and break over Calvin Rutherford's body. He dissolved, only some traces of flesh, bone and clothing left by the time rescue arrived—too late.

Once again the afternoon papers were somehow hijacked and a picture of Calvin Rutherford, his skull and bones stark in black and white for all to see. Beneath the huge, horrific photograph, another headline read:

X DEFEATED AGAIN. WILL HE LOSE A THIRD TIME?

Another death at your feet, you have until morning to rescue the next victim. Bell, book, and candle shall not drive me back, when gold and silver beckons me to come on.

Agent X read the paper for a fifth time, having left the scene of the Mayor's death disguised as a beat cop. Burks had ordered him to secure the perimeter and when a similar looking officer came on the scene, X passed the job on and left. He already knew the poor man died by the acid torture, an old and terrible form of death invented by certain evil gangs in the streets of Florence. The fact that Madam Rogue used this means of murder was unsurprising. The fiend loved horrific deaths, spreading terror to all. In the past she'd killed people with plague infested mice and similar terrible ways of spreading death to her victims. No, that he understood and accepted.

But this method of teasing, riddling and using the same method each time to announce her crimes. This was too routine for the criminal genius. Madam Rogue was considered, even by her opponents to possess a first class mind, albeit one twisted with evil. Her actions caused whole nations to quake with fear. These attacks, while well-planned and wicked, did not possess that spark of genius that the master criminal always demonstrated.

Agent X nodded his head, having an idea on that subject but not willing to devote any further time to the subject. He needed to stop the next crime before it occurred, but this time he wasn't caught ignorant of the subject.

His private line chimed a number that was untraceable and changed every week. Only a rare few men and women had this number and they only called when the situation was dire.

Picking up the receiver, he waited, never starting these conversations. Betty's nearly breathless voice came through the line. "I know the quote this time too! It's from…"

"*King John* by William Shakespeare," X replied, cutting her off. "The least read, least known play by the man. I know. I will take care of that end. I have a different assignment for you."

Betty was slightly disappointed that X knew the quote already, but that feeling lasted only a few seconds. He had an assignment for her, which was rare and usually very dangerous. "What do you need?"

Secret Agent X smiled slightly, hearing the excitement in Betty's voice. If there was anyone in the world he could devote his life to loving, it would be this woman. But that fate was not meant to be, Agent X had a different lot in life. His life was devoted to the battle against evil and that was a road one traveled alone.

"Somehow Madam Rogue is changing the front pages of your paper and the other two in town. This was not accomplished by magic. No, this was performed by human hands. She is either controlling or threatening one or more employees at each paper. Find out who is her victim or helper at your paper. Then we can get a step ahead of her and find out her next murder plan." Agent X explained as he scanned the list he'd been compiling earlier. One name fit the profile of Madam Rogue's attacks this time.

"Should I call you when I find out? Or should I call the police?" Betty asked thinking of the men who worked on the pressing floor and wondering who could have access to such sensitive material. The creation of a headline and front page wasn't a simple exercise and required a great deal of skill.

"Send the information to my drop box. Call John Burks or Charlie Foster with the information. But be careful! Madam Rogue never leaves her minions or servants alone. They're watched and she is always prepared to destroy them if they get in her way." X explained as he pocketed a keen throwing knife and his gas gun. With those final words, he applied the finishing touches to his disguise and left his headquarters. Madam Rogue's victim could right now being tortured and there was still time to save a life!

Arthur Wade was not a happy man, not even a little bit. Nothing was every placed in its proper place and everything was far too untidy. Running a pristine white glove over the top rim of a display case, he discovered another layer of dust all along the back edge. Heads would roll for this failure; he would ensure that some people would lose their jobs tomorrow!

The head curator of the Natural History museum, Wade demanded a level of cleanliness that was considered impossible by the staff. Every case, every item on all four floors of the huge structure must be dusted and cleaned three times daily, with the white glove treatment performed randomly throughout the day. Three failures to ensure the exhibits were sparkling would result in a suspension. A fourth would mean the offender would be fired without a recommendation.

Why did the museum put up with a man so demanding, so ready to angrily insult trained professionals for missing one fingerprint on a case? Simply because Arthur Wade was a master at creating exhibitions that would ensure huge grants for the museum. His ability to determine which area to highlight enabled this museum to remain a place of learning even when other similar institutions were struggling to keep their doors open.

Arthur Wade was a tall, thin man with a full head of mousy brown hair and a perfectly clipped brush-like mustache. His clothes always looked perfect and it was rumored he kept a full closet of exact duplicates of his outfits to replace any that became dusty or stained. The rumor was true, but in fact he kept three copies of everything he wore at work and had an additional two closets full of duplicates in case of fraying or stains. The idea of dirt on any surface caused Arthur Wade to fill with rage and he was determined that every aspect of his life would be sterile and pristine.

The current exhibition was one of his finest works to date, one that many of the board had been surprised Wade proposed as the lead. The exposition was entitled, "Coins Through History", a subject that could have been quite sterile and dull. But not under Arthur Wade. No way. He created a series of exhibits that were not merely rows upon rows of coins with little typed cards. No, they created dioramas showing great and thrilling moments that involved the use of coins throughout time.

For example, when anyone walked in, they were greeted by a larger than life Blackbeard the Pirate burying a chest of doubloons, jewels and other riches. Three dead men lay at his feet, while another cowered in terror as the pirate raised his saber to strike. This scene alone fascinated most of the public and it was only the first one could see upon entry.

Why did he created such a unique expo for a subject that most concerned to be a dull hobby? Simple: this attracted a very wealthy patron to the museum who was delighted to lend a small piece of his huge collection.

And he was also donating money to build a new wing for the museum, something that thrilled the board of trustees. In their eyes, Arthur Wade was the reason the museum was flourishing when others were struggling for funds.

Stepping before the diorama of a band of thuggish-looking Gaul warriors surrounding a party of elderly-looking Roman nobles. Brennus, the chief of the Gauls, was pointing his sword at the complaining Senators, who were piling stacks of coins at the huge warlord's feet. Pulling out a white glove, Wade ran a hand all along the surfaces of the case and smiled as his glove was still pristine. Young Mr. Allen was assigned to this section and he did seem to understand the proper way to run his areas. Proper placement of all figures, clean cases with no fingerprints on the glass and clear, simply written explanations of the scene. These were more important than long and dull research papers like that Phipps of the dinosaur floor. That man seemed to view exact details of his bones, long research papers and trips as the most important parts of the museum. Honestly, who cared if the Tyrannosaurus Rex was extinct long before the saber-toothed tiger? It looked good to the public and that was why there was a museum after all.

Walking over to the diorama of King Henry VIII paying the executioner of his now headless wife Anne Boleyn, Wade ran his glove along the surfaces and nodded. Yes, Allen was doing very, very well and would be his choice for the next assistant curator posts in the museum. If only he could get rid of Phipps, but the man's many awards and discoveries made him untouchable, for now.

Pulling out his favorite fountain pen and leather-bound notebook, Arthur Wade wrote a few lines in praise of Allen. Later he would dictate this information to his secretary and a memo would go out, telling all that Allen was getting the available promotion because of his excellent behavior and service. This would be an example to others and hopefully they would shape up and begin working more in line with Arthur Wade's methods for the museum.

Just after placing an exactly round period at the end of the future memo a large hand clamped a cloth over his nose and mouth. A second hand encircled Wade's throat and the museum official opened his mouth, attempting to scream. But in doing so he accidentally inhaled and a harsh scent entered his nose and mouth. Wade found his body weakening, his arms slowly dropping to his sides. His expensive fountain pen clattered to the ground along with his notebook just as blackness entered the corners of his vision. A few seconds later he knew no more and collapsed, his attacker lifting him with ease.

The woman in the black hood dropped Arthur Wade to the ground. This death would be a masterpiece and the coins present were a perfect robbery. This would be Madam Rogue's most terrifying headline and the infamous Secret Agent X would be helpless to save this victim as well!

Betty Dale tapped her pen on her desk and thought. *Who could best create the front page secretly and replace the original?* There weren't many people who had access to those areas, despite the large number of people working on the press floor. This was a highly skilled job, creating the plate that would produce the paper in mass quantities. But in this case the best method would be to start with Jake Wells, the head of the pressing floor.

Betty knew Wells, a huge balding man with salt and pepper hair, a love of cigars with a racing form perpetually in his hands or a back pocket. He was a loud, blustery type, but very good at his job. If he wasn't involved, he'd know which of his team would have access to the equipment necessary to assist Madam Rogue in her plans.

Picking up her pocket book, Betty walked down to the basement level ignoring the looks of surprise she received from some of the men. They all knew Betty Dale, the lovely top reporter who was the object of many a male fantasy. But seeing her down in their area was a surprise that had them all staring and wondering what to do next.

Betty solved the problem by walking straight up to Jake Wells, who was ignoring her and studying the racing form. He circled a horse with a well-chewed pencil and puffed out a small stream of smoke from his thin cigar. Betty glanced at his choice and chuckled out loud, shaking her head.

"I guess it's true," she said with a laugh, "gamblers all prefer to lose money. Why don't you just toss your cash out the window and save time?"

"Ha?" Jake Wells asked, his narrow green eyes lifting and focusing on the lithe form of Betty Dale. Her frowned, seeing her being in his domain as something out-of-place and very strange.

"You chose a horse owned by Rick Liefer and ridden by Sy Ormand. Liefer is about the unluckiest guy on the planet. And Sy Ormand is so crooked he's practically the local mob boss's personal jockey." Betty replied with an ironic smile.

"How do you know so much about the ponies?" Wells asked, interested despite himself.

"The horses? I wouldn't know one end from the other. But I wrote a story on the city jockey club and learned a lot of insider gossip I wasn't allowed to print." Betty explained and shook her head. The jockeys, trainers, and officials had fallen all over themselves attempting to tell stories that would impress her. Sadly all were just that, stories, and she'd been unable to prove the details enough to pass the editors.

"Can I help you, Miss Dale?" Wells grumped, moving his cigar from one end of his mouth to another. He smelled of cigar smoke and stale whiskey and seemed irritated at the beautiful reporter's presence as well as her knowledge of the people in racing.

"Yes," Betty replied, unimpressed by Wells's attempting to intimidate her by his large presence. She'd faced professional killers, living dead men and monsters that would cause even the bravest men to shriek in terror. A large press foreman wasn't going to impress her, not after all the adventures she'd undergone with Secret Agent X. "Perhaps in your office?"

Wells frowned even deeper, looking as if he wanted to argue. But he finally nodded and led her across the floor to a small wooden and glass chamber with a battered metal desk. Sitting down behind the desk with a sigh, he dropped his racing form on the top and said in a growling voice, "I can give you five minutes. What's your problem?"

"The front pages are being changed. That's not an easy job. I'd like to know how it's happening." Betty answered, sitting on the edge of the wooden chair gripping her handbag tightly.

"Like I told the police," Wells grumbled, "I don't know. It ain't possible."

Betty shook her head, "It's quite possible if the person committing the crimes had the headlines planned in advance. The plate could be prepared and the photograph inserted last. Then simply place that one in and replace the one planned by the editor."

"Not without my knowledge!" Wells snapped, leaning his elbows against the desk and looking down on the attractive young reporter.

"Exactly," Betty Dale replied and smiled broadly. She knew this wasn't an admission, but catching Wells stating that he was the only man who could perform this act made life far easier. "Were you threatened, or paid? I'm guessing, based on your skill at picking horses, a bribe would be all you need. How much were you given? Maybe, $500 with a promise of another $500 once this was done. How close am I?"

Wells stood up and slammed a fist on the desk top, "I didn't take no bribe! You can't prove nothing! Get out of here you stuck-up little liar!"

Betty didn't move, but smiled wider, "I've always found when someone tells me I can't prove something, they're as guilty as sin. I think a phone call to Inspector John Burks is in order. I'm guessing a search of your place

"I didn't take no bribe!"

will reveal a poorly hidden stash of money and enough evidence to send you up the river for a long time. Then again, the DA might see you as being involved, which could mean the chair."

Wells's ruddy face turned purple with rage and he stepped around the desk, one huge fist balling while the other opened and closed, "No way you're gonna get me sent to some cell! I'll kill you first!"

As Wells stepped closer, Betty Dale slipped off her chair and swung her pocket book up in a fast arc. The leather purse struck the huge man under the chin with a sickening thud and sent him flying backwards against the wooden and glass wall. He collapsed to the ground, his jaw twisted and his eyes rolling back in his head.

How did Betty Dale knock out a man roughly three times her size with a simple pocket book? Simple enough thanks to Secret Agent X. The Man of Mystery was an expert at the creation and use of hidden weapons. Realizing that Betty might be placed in a dangerous situation where she didn't have time to draw and use a firearm, he designed a very special pocket book. The leather covered a half inch of a steel alloy that was light-weight but incredibly hard. A hard swing by Betty, who was taught how to use the weapon by Agent X, was like getting hit in the face by a baseball bat. But since the area of the purse was smaller, the results were nothing short of devastating.

Betty stepped over the fallen body and reached for the phone, dialing the switchboard operator. "Outside line please, Ernestine." she asked.

"Yes, Miss Dale. Slumming are you today? Perhaps when you're done there you'll take a tour of skid row for your next date!" The nasal voiced switchboard operator inquired and snorted several times. You could almost hear the sneer in the woman's voice and Betty winced at the sound. She'd heard Ernestine had a daughter too, terrifying thought. Probably a future telephone operator too.

"Very amusing, I'm sure." Betty replied and heard the click as the outside line was connected and she dialed for the operator. Hearing the operator's voice, she was about to give Inspector John Burks's number when the door opened behind her. Looking up, her mouth dropped in surprise as Phil Pulver walked into the office. In his hands was a large pistol!

"Put down the receiver, Betty. Oh and drop that nasty purse to the ground. I'm not an idiot like Wells over there," Pulver sneered and nodded towards the pocket book in her other hand.

Betty frowned as she dropped the telephone back onto the cradle and shook her head. She pushed the purse off the desk, causing it to land with a heavy thunk near Pulver's feet. "I might have known you were in this with Wells. He wouldn't have thought of this on his own."

Pulver, a tall thin man with a shock of salt and pepper hair and tiny blue eyes, glanced down at the fallen Wells. His face was covered with a day's growth of beard and there were heavy circles under both of his eyes. He always looked harried and tired to Betty, but until this moment he'd appeared an effective editor for the newspaper. Not particularly inspired, but good at producing a quality paper twice daily.

Now there was something off about the man, as if the worst characteristics of him had taken over and there was nothing else left. Pulver appeared a rumpled, ineffective little man, a pathetic figure whose only strength was the pistol in his hand. Betty almost felt sorry for the man. Almost. It was obvious to her that he was a coward, one bolstered by the gun in his hand.

"That's right! Wells was just my flunky! I was the one approached first and I told the way to mysteriously replace the front pages. I'm already rich and afterwards I'll be even richer!" Pulver bragged, raising the gun up.

"How will you explain shooting me? I don't care how much money you have, you can't explain that to the police!" Betty asked, trying to buy time and find a way out of the mess she was in.

"I won't have to! The presses are about to start and the noise down here will be too loud for anyone to hear a hundred gunshots. I'll just shoot you and put the gun in Wells's hand and he'll die in prison or the chair. I don't particularly care either way." Pulver bragged and smiled a crooked, stain toothed smile.

Betty smiled back and grabbed the telephone, throwing it at Pulver's face. He started and moved to block the telephone, giving Betty enough time to dive beneath the desk. Pulver fired once, the bullet striking the wall and causing splinters to fly around the room.

"This room is a small box, Dale. You can't escape for long!" Pulver crowed, raising the gun and stepping slowly around the desk. He pushed the heavy, dangerous pocket book towards the door in case getting it was part of Betty Dale's plans.

But Betty was far more resourceful than Phil Pulver could possibly know. The minute she dove to the ground, she pulled out Jake Well's desk drawers, having an idea what she'd find. She wasn't disappointed; a half full bottle of rotgut whiskey lay on the bottom drawer next to a nearly empty box of cigars and kitchen matches. She grabbed the bottle and two more objects. Sliding back away from Pulver, she quickly prepared to strike.

"Trying to crawl away, Dale? I'm disappointed! You were always renown for your courage and fearlessness. People said you were tougher than most men! Yet here you are, crawling around the floor, like a pathetic little dog. I knew you didn't have it in you!" Pulver stated, his voice full of derision as he stalked closer.

In response, Betty tossed the cigar box towards the door, knowing Pulver would react. Like all men inexperienced with a gun, he startled easily and reacted to every noise. Spinning towards the noise he fired his gun, striking the door and chipping the heavy wood.

It was then that Betty struck! In her hand was the whiskey bottle with a lit handkerchief in the mouth. She threw it with all her strength at Phil Pulver watching as it shattered and caused the now flaming alcohol to cover his body. He shrieked in fear and pain, collapsing to the ground as he screamed. Betty ran across the room and grabbed Jake Wells's over coat. Tossing it on Pulver and beginning to put out the flames. Then she grabbed her purse and the gun before reaching for the fallen telephone again.

"Ernestine? Get me the police. Inspector John Burks, actually. And I don't have time for any banter. This is a matter of life and death!" Betty stated, cutting off the nasal voiced switchboard operator before the taunting began.

Arthur Wade was an even more unhappy man than usual. He awoke a short time after the terrible chemicals on the cloth knocked him out, only to find himself in a worse situation. He was tied up with his mouth gagged and laying in a large box made of wood and metal. On top of the box near his feet was a large clock with a swinging pendulum. The clock made a loud ticking sound, counting off the seconds with each swing of the brass arm.

Every time the clock's big hand moved, indicating a minute passing, the box compressed a short distance. At first the feeling wasn't unpleasant but with each tick of the clock, the box pressed him in more and more. It was then that Wade realized that the box would compress into that of a small cube, one in which he would be a shattered, destroyed bag of flesh. The slow agonies would be monstrous and there would be little of him left by the end.

Wade struggled in vain to pull himself free and attempted to scream, all to no avail. He stared at the clock, wincing with each tick of the mechanism, the sound getting louder in his mind with each second. He tried to concentrate on the ceiling, examining every square inch above him and attempting to find anything out of place. But the tick-tock, tick-tock of the clock intruded into his thoughts with each second. It was like a relentless drumming, a thrumming that surrounded his whole being and was driving him to madness.

A soft footfall intruded over the sound and a moment later a man appeared in his vision. He was of medium height with light blonde hair and a nondescript face that was easily forgotten. Arthur Wade attempted to break free of his bonds, to scream through his gag, terrified that this was the man who was the source of his torment. But the man didn't move any closer, in fact he appeared to be ignoring Wade and studying the mechanism.

"Stay still," the man commanded, not looking at Wade. He had a low, gruff voice that was very commanding in its tone.

Despite himself, Arthur Wade stopped struggling against his bonds, sensing this man may be the route to his salvation. The man's gaze was unwavering; he seemed to be taking in every detail of the machine. Wade merely wished he would get on with it!

"There is a block of a very powerful explosive beneath your head. If I free you, your body or your mouth, that will ignite. Please remain quite still and I will attempt to disarm the death trap," Agent X stated pulling out a miniature tool kit he always kept handy.

Arthur Wade froze in place, attempting to keep his breathing under control. Explosives under his body? A machine pressing him into a small cube? Was this a penny dreadful? He began, despite himself, to hyperventilate. The fear of death filled his very soul. Wade finally succumbed to fear of the trap and passed out, slumped in place and breathing lightly.

Secret Agent X nodded, grateful that the man wasn't struggling any further. Had he continued to attempt to free himself, X was prepared to use his gas gun on the man to subdue him. This was an intricate trap in many ways, a classic compression machine attached to a clockwork mechanism. Interesting, but not as ingenious as he had assumed Madam Rogue would create. This confirmed his beliefs, but that was not important at the moment.

Following the connecting wire from the clock to the gears that tightened the mechanism, the Agent spotted a second wire that connected the clock to the plastic explosives beneath Wade's body. There was also a third wire that ran from the clockwork mechanism to the bomb, a simple circuit. If he cut any of the connections, the bomb would explode. Fiendish, but also fairly rudimentary.

Rolling his eyes, Agent X climbed beneath Wade's strapped body and spotted the ignition circuit. As he expected it was connected to both the clockwork and the bomb, but that was it. Not much of a death trap in fact. Oh, this would be very fatal to anyone who wasn't experienced at such situations. But Agent X, he was one of the world's greatest experts on the subject.

In a few moments he disconnected the circuits connected to the bomb, unstrapped Arthur Wade and lay the poor man aside. He then switched off the clockwork machine and searched the area, finding exactly what he expected. Pulling out a small round tube, he tapped the buttons on the side and smiled as all of the alarms in the building went off at once. A useful device, one that he'd been saving for just such an occasion. Within minutes the museum would be filled with the local and state police, not to mention the fire department and other rescue agencies. Arthur Wade would be taken care of and Madam Rogue was beaten this round at least.

The trap wasn't up to Madam Rogue's standards. The woman is a fiend, a horrific monster who loved to cause pain in her victims. This trap, while terrible, was the work of an imitator. I wonder... Secret Agent X thought as he exited the museum and hopped into his roadster. It was time to get back to his headquarters and do a little research.

Betty Dale was quite happy at this time; she was just finishing her story about tracking down the source of the headlines. The temporary editor wanted every detail, including how she flattened both Jake Wells and Phil Pulver. The actual details had to be edited down somewhat, but the result was she was looking at possibly receiving several awards and a raise in pay from the publishers.

"Copy!" She yelled out and the runner came to her side, accepting her story and running to the editor's desk. Betty spotted Richmond nearby, glowering her direction as he got ready to leave to write the story Pulver had previously assigned to her; a lady's garden party for the society page. And he would be on such assignments for a good long time, the publishers and editors were disgusted that he hadn't tracked down the story Betty just presented.

Getting up and heading to the ladies room, Betty Dale locked the door behind her and walked to the third stall. Closing the stall behind her, she pressed a hand on the fourth tile above the tank, causing the ceramic square to recede into the wall. She then tapped several tiles in a pattern and watched as the original square slid aside. Reaching in, she pulled out a small metal tube, in which she inserted a fold of paper. This was the information Betty promised Secret Agent X and this was the first time since the attack by Pulver that she was able to get here and send it. The last thing she or X needed was John Burks or Charlie Foster wondering why she was lingering in the ladies room. Returning the metal tube back into the wall, she heard it shoot away, a private pneumatic tube system hidden throughout the city and used only by the aides of Secret Agent X.

Heading back to her desk, Betty immediately began working on a follow-up story, grateful for the quotes Foster gave her before they carted off Wells and Pulver. Both were probably being interrogated in the lowest cells by Burks himself, determined to capture the one he believed was behind the murders: Secret Agent X. It wouldn't be long before the other two papers were free of accomplices to the mastermind behind these attacks; Foster was determined to catch them that afternoon. He promised Betty the exclusive, which was why she was preparing the story in advance. The names and jobs of the men involved would be filled in later and her paper would be the toast of the city.

Just then her phone chimed and she picked it up, wondering if Foster was that quick. "Betty Dale, how may I help you?"

"You know who this is," an odd metallic voice stated, "we spoke earlier today and you told me about a famous book."

Despite the harsh sounding voice, Betty smiled, "Yes, I do remember. I've heard that poor museum curator was rescued. That will be the smaller story on the front page."

"Understood. I am about to capture the mastermind behind these attacks. I need your help and you will have an even better story. Meet me at this address..."

Betty's eyebrows rose, "You're about to capture Madam Rogue? Okay, I'll be there!" she replied and jotted down the address. She then yelled for the copy boy again and added, "Tell them Commissioner Foster will be calling soon and will supply the names and positions of the other conspirators. I have a lead to follow!"

Before the copy boy could reply, Betty grabbed her purse and was off, running for the stairs. The capture of Madam Rogue by Secret Agent X was just an incredible adventure! The fact that it could lead to a Pulitzer Prize winning story was neither here nor there in her mind. Her first priority was always helping the man she adored, Secret Agent X.

Agent X examined his files on criminals of the world, still astonished by the sheer volume of mad geniuses on Earth. The file for Dr. Satan alone was almost a full file cabinet thick. Despite all the information on the man, they still didn't know the his identity. He might be a bored millionaire with the mind of a scientist, but he might be an inhuman being who came to this world intent on spreading chaos. There was no way to know and X didn't have time to explore the different avenues.

The Madam Rogue file was far smaller, more of a list of crimes and rumors. The woman was just too intelligent, too expert at not getting caught. The one time she was believed to have been caught by German authorities and executed by the hanging proved false. Somehow the woman put in a duplicate and returned to her horrific crimes against humanity, starting with brutally murdering all of the detectives who almost brought about her end. There were a few notes from X, written after the Great War, but they were unimportant. In the end it was the rumors he read, tales of the woman's interests, lovers, family and the like. Agent X circled several lines and nodded, glad to see his beliefs based on the current murders were true.

Changing into another identity, he was about to leave his headquarters when the pneumatic tube from the newspaper arrived. Sliding open the pipe, he pulled out the small metal tube that carried the messages. Inside was a small folded note, no doubt the information Betty promised to deliver. Unfortunately, he could not be more wrong in this respect. The note was written in block letters and the contents caused a catch in his throat.

> *Well done, my creation. You have saved one and cut off my means of terrifying the city. This is a temporary victory for you, enjoy it. I shall soon remove from you your heart and you shall wish to die by my hand. You have one hour. The city aquarium. Come alone. MR.*

Secret Agent X balled the note in his fist, his eyes blazing with fury. The monster captured Betty Dale, that was what the note was conveying. She wanted to execute Betty in front of Agent X as a way of hurting him as well as a means of proving who was the master. But she would not succeed, because Secret Agent X would rescue Betty Dale and destroy this terrible fiend once and for all!

Grabbing several items, X was out the door in no time flat, jumping into his fastest roadster and heading to the city aquarium. He had an idea what this monster was planning. If his theory was right, this woman's reign of terror over the city was close to ending!

The city aquarium was usually a bustling location and a favorite spot for tourists and local families. It wasn't a particular large place and didn't possess a massive number of animals. But it was a bright, cheery location that welcomed visitors and allowed them to see sights both astonishing and terrifying. There were regular fundraisers to keep the place running, with new animals added each year to keep up excitement. Generally during a bright sunny day such as this one, there were long lines to get in since the admission price was just a nickel, affordable by even the poorest families in the city.

But not today. The aquarium was closed; apparently one of the tanks was in danger of rupturing. Even the security guards were sent home by order, leaving the place an empty shell. The caretakers fed all the animals before leaving and left, some grumbling that they would be hopelessly behind in their work tomorrow when the buildings reopened.

Agent X parked his car near the gate and ran inside, stopping only to consult a large map. Finding the location he sought, he sprinted across the park, ignoring the sounds of seals barking and other joyful things that filled the park. No, he was going to the darkest part of the park, the area which was meant to terrify visitors and give them a chill they would speak about for years. X was heading for the shark tank, the most popular section of the park by far. Men, women and children came to get a glimpse of one of the most dangerous creatures in the world.

The shark tank, to visitors, was a dark building entered through a long line and taking them into a circular room whose center was an enormous glass enclosed tank. The sharks circled about the tank, apparently oblivious to the staring humans, eating when fed and always moving. Occasionally one of the sharks, the fierce creatures known as Tiger Sharks, would move close to the glass, causing visitors to shriek and leap backwards, even though there was no chance whatsoever for them to break free.

The sharks themselves were enormous creatures, the smallest being a ten foot male and the largest a twelve foot female that the keepers called "Bertha". Feeding time for these creatures was one of the favorite periods each day, with the sharks going into a frenzy as they circled and tore into the bloody meat they were given. There was something fascinating, watching these nearly prehistorical creatures attacking their food. The keepers of the aquarium knew all too well their biggest draw and used these sharks as a means of funding the whole park.

But Agent X didn't go anywhere near the visiting area, his target was in a far more dangerous location. Leaping over the "Employees Only, Keep Out" barrier, he ran up a flight of stairs, through an open door and entered an unlit corridor. Pulling out his gas gun and palming a throwing knife, X slowly walked down the hallway. His enemy probably hadn't brought any help, but one never knew. Better to be careful and safe. Failure to do so could cost Betty Dale's life!

Happily the hallway was clear, empty of all life and smelling strongly of drying blood and fish. This was where the keepers carried the bloody fish they fed to the sharks and there were no closets of offices off the hallway. Despite being very clean, the corridor smelled strongly of death and decay, a sickly scent that reminded secret Agent X of the war and the terrible smells that hit everyone once they entered a zone where men died. As a warrior against evil, Agent X experienced these scents all too many times, but his controlled mind suppressed any visions of the past. He needed all his concentration to be focused on saving the life of Betty Dale.

Stepping out of the hallway, X was now in a huge circular chamber, nearly the full size of the building itself. The most obvious feature was the circular container of water, the shark tank itself. A scent of salt water mixed with the bloody smells Agent X experienced earlier, it was an odd combination known only to men who fought battles at sea. The tank's water was blue and moved slowly, as if a light current ran through the shark's aquarium. The sharks were not visible, but X sensed their deadly presence just beneath the surface of the water.

A large metal frame surrounded the tank with many signs indicating the proper method to feed the sharks and how best to avoid danger. The hazard of falling into a tank of Tiger Sharks was a clear and present danger every time the keepers entered this chamber; therefore the aquarium management was determined to make it clear that violating the rules would place workers at great risk.

But Agent X wasn't interested in the walkway or the signs. His interest was at the far end of the room. Across the way was Betty Dale, her golden blonde hair shining like a halo in the grim chamber. Her bright eyes were wild with fear, an understandable emotion given her circumstances.

The beautiful Betty Dale was trussed to a huge anchor with thick rope, it was easily twice the size of her lithe form. The anchor, dangling above the shark tank, was attached to a huge rusted chain leading to a well-used wench. Standing behind the winch was a woman in black, her black leather gloved hand gripping the control handle. The woman in black's face was covered with a heavy dark hood, one in which her eyes were barely visible.

Agent X knew this was one of the many looks Madam Rogue used to hide her identity. But that had been the only identity the fiend had used this time. For a murderous thief who was a master of disguise, her actions

...Betty Dale was trussed...to a huge anchor...

had been quite limited and unimpressive. This fit Secret Agent X's theories, but he didn't have time to consider such details at this moment.

"Move no further," Madam Rogue stated, her voice sounding tinny and mechanical. X noticed there was no movement around the facial area of the black hood, which was interesting as well.

X stopped in his tracks and waited, pushing the knife back up his sleeve. His other hand still held his gas gun, extended and ready to fire. The distance was far too great, but Agent X was prepared to do whatever it took to save Betty Dale from her terrible fate. At the moment, control of the situation was in the hands of Madam Rogue. Secret Agent X was forced to wait for the madwoman to act first. X did not like being in a position of reacting to a criminal, but at the moment he had no choice.

"Throw your gas gun and the knife attached to your leg in the water. Slowly! Failure to do so will result in the immediate death of your Miss Dale." Madam Rogue stated, her voice still that inhuman buzz that grated on the nerves.

Agent X nodded once and tossed the gas gun into the shark tank and slowly squatted down. He pulled out the throwing knife he'd kept attached to his right leg since the Great War, a holdout weapon he learned from Madam Rogue himself in those days. Originally he'd scoffed at the idea of a holdout blade, but the evil mastermind proved correct in her assertion that it was a good, fast means of remaining armed at all times. More than a few times enemies failed to feel the back of his calf and missed the knife, giving Agent X a weapon to begin their path to destruction.

Standing up, X tossed the weapon into the shark tank and looked up at the madwoman holding Betty hostage. Agent X wanted to say something, but he fought back the urge. It would be best to let the fiend control the situation, until it was time to turn things around.

"I would not recognize you," Madam Rogue intoned, her hooded head moving left and right as she examined Secret Agent X. "Your skills have grown since you betrayed me and attempted to destroy me!"

Agent X shook his head, "I never betrayed you." he replied.

"You did!" Madam Rogue's mechanical voice rose slightly, but otherwise remained the same robotic noise. "You stabbed me and threw me from a bridge in Paris!"

Agent X chuckled without a trace of humor, "Thank you."

Madam Rogue tilted his head to the right, "Why do you thank me? I am about to destroy you out of revenge! I will kill the woman of your heart and you will be helpless to save her from a brutal, horrible end!"

Secret Agent X smiled, showing his teeth in a grin in imitation of the sharks below their feet. "Because you just confirmed to me that you're not Madam Rogue. I knew these attacks were just imitations of past ones performed by that fiendish genius. But there was always the possibility that the world's greatest criminal was no longer the evil, imaginative mastermind of past days. Now you're proven yourself to not be Madam Rogue."

"Liar! I am the one and only Madam Rogue! I am the terror of mankind, the shadow of fear. I am Madam Rogue!" Madam Rogue stated, her mechanical voice rising to denote a raised voice but still sounding inhuman.

"First, Madam Rogue never spoke in that manner. The woman had, or maybe has, far too much dignity to speak in such a grandiose style. Second, I never stabbed Madam Rogue or threw her from a bridge in Paris. I shot her in a sewer in Vienna, igniting gases in the tunnels. She was believed killed, but we never found a body or heard from her again. I spread the other story so that Allied Intelligence knew the real monster from false ones. There were five or six that stepped forward, claiming to be Madam Rogue. I believe two were imprisoned for other crimes and the others were executed for crimes they committed."

"What? What?" The woman calling herself Madam Rogue asked, confusion coming through even with her mechanical voice. "You are lying!"

Agent X shook his head, "I wouldn't bother. I just wanted you to know that I'm not impressed. I'm guessing you're one of Madam Rogue's daughters, maybe the one called Thalia. I heard somewhere she was shot, possibly in the throat. Based on your voice, you appear to have bought or stolen the musical voice technology by that murderous maniac, Phibes. I'm guessing you stole the machine since my information holds that Phibes sounded quite human. You sound like a tin toy with a broken spring."

The woman calling herself Madam Rogue stared at Agent X for a full minute before reaching up and pulling off her hood. The woman beneath proved to be completely hairless, her face a pale skull with flesh pulled across a round head. Her eyes were long, wide and possessing narrow red pupils. The sockets of her eyes seemed too large for her head, giving the woman an inhuman, bestial look. There was a narrow black wire attached to her throat, running down her torso to a small box near her belt.

"You are correct, sir. I am one of the legendary Madam Rogue's daughters. She executed any sons she bore and few of her children survived. And I have heard of her pupil, the Man of a Thousand Faces, Secret Agent X. Or should I call you..?" The daughter of Madam Rogue asked, but was cut off by a chopping gesture by Agent X.

"The name you are about to use was just an alias, one we used to place Madam Rogue at ease. I doubt she believed that was my name. And I don't care what you call me; we're not friends or colleagues. I intend to rescue Betty Dale and capture you. Unlike your so-called parent, you won't escape justice." Secret Agent X snapped back, not allowing this monster to attempt to befriend him. That was the way of madmen and women, they wished to cause their enemies to believe they were alike. This caused many to lower their guard and get killed. Agent X would never fall victim to such a mistake.

"Oh do you? If you survive, see me at France's Folly and we shall battle once and for all!" The daughter of Madam Rogue stated and pulled the lever on the winch.

The chain immediately began to slip and the anchor fell into the shark tank with a loud splash. The daughter of Madam Rogue watched as the chain followed the anchor into the tank and stepped away. In a quick movement, she vaulted out of the nearby window and out of sight a moment later.

Secret Agent X ran along the walkway, stopping near where Betty was dropped. Kicking off his shoes and pulling a pair or goggles over his eyes, he gently slipped into the water. The temptation to dive in and swim to Betty's side was great, but foolish. Diving and swimming frantically would attract the attention of the sharks, even more so than the anchor holding Betty.

Placing a metal tube in his mouth, he swam down with quick efficient strokes. He spotted Betty immediately and saw one of the sharks was circling not to far away. It was bad; the creatures had a sense of smell far greater than humans and could smell a helpless, dying victim. They were the apex predators of the ocean, feared by nearly all marine life because they were dangerous, efficient hunters and killers.

Reaching Betty's side mere seconds later, he pulled off the gag on her mouth and placed a similar tube in her mouth. Holding her nose, she inhaled at the tube, instantly breathing in clean, if slightly stale air. Her eyes were still wild with fear, but at least she now knew she could breathe. The fact that she was tied to an anchor and surrounded by hungry Tiger Sharks still had her terrified. But with Secret Agent X present, at least she had a chance of surviving.

Agent X had less faith in his skills at that moment than Betty Dale, but he pushed doubt to the back of his mind. He knew there were three sharks in the tank and they were all hungry. The nearest one was circling and, based on his past experiences with such predators, would make a run their direction soon. Pulling out the knife he kept up his sleeve, X knew his blade was a toy compared to the jaws of a shark, but he had no choice. For Betty's sake he needed to defeat these predators!

The shark circling suddenly turned X's direction, swimming in a straight line towards them. X tried to move aside, but wasn't fast enough. His right arm hit the shark; the sleeve of his shirt was shredded. Blood welled from the arm and he felt a sharp, biting pain, the skin of the shark was like sandpaper!

The situation was more dangerous since now there was fresh blood in the water. This would drive the sharks mad with bloodlust and imperiled Agent X and Betty Dale more than they had been a moment earlier!

Just then X was hit from behind by the flank of a second shark, one he hadn't spotted in the murk of the tank. Agent X bit back a scream of pain as his back was torn open by the skin of the second shark. Backing, he spotted the two sharks that attacked him, but the third was still not visible. The two were now circling in a tighter pattern, Betty no longer being their target. Agent X, bleeding and injured was now the prey.

The shark that surprised him suddenly changed direction, heading straight for Agent X. The creature's rows of sharp teeth flashed in the gloom as it swam with lethal intent towards Secret Agent X. If the tiger shark bit X, there was little chance he could survive. The creature and the other two sharks would tear him to pieces in mere seconds!

But Agent X had no intention of being the dinner of a fish, even one of the most efficiently dangerous ones on the planet. Blowing all of the air out of his lungs, X pushed his arms up fast and dropped beneath the shark, missing the monstrous creature's teeth and abrasive skin by mere inches. He didn't bother trying to swing his knife at the shark's underbelly. Unlike some animals, shark's skins are tough underneath and X's blade wouldn't scratch monstrous beast.

It was then that the third shark appeared, the largest one known as Bertha to the keepers and the public. More monstrous than the other two, she was larger by several feet over the other two. Turning Agent X's direction, her enormous maw was visible even from a distance. Bertha the shark swam with the speed of an arrow, aimed for X, determined to tear him apart in one attack.

This was Agent X's one chance to survive the encounter and rescue Betty Dale. Facing Bertha, he gripped the knife with a hand so tight his knuckles turned white. Following the shark's speedy progress, he quickly moved to the side and as it was almost upon him he stabbed out with his blade. The wicked blade hit the shark's exposed gills, slicing them open and causing a cloud of blood to appear in the water. The huge shark circled down, thrashing in agony as it swam in random directions.

Then one of the other sharks struck, but not at Agent X. The blood streaming from the wounded shark drove the others into a frenzy and the smaller shark bit down on the exposed, injured flank of the larger. The second uninjured shark attacked the other side and the larger shark thrashed about in its death throes.

Seeing a chance to escape, Agent X dove down quickly towards Betty, swimming with long but gentle strokes. The last thing he wanted was to create a disturbance in the water and attract the attention of the blood crazed sharks. Arriving at Betty's side, he quickly sliced her bonds, grabbed her waist and pushed off the floor of the tank.

Within a few seconds they were on the surface and Agent X pushed Betty onto the deck. He pulled himself up a moment later and lay on the floor, breathing heavily and feeling the throbbing pain in his arm and back.

"Thank you," Betty panted, taking Agent X's hand. "I thought I was done for! What did you put in my mouth to get me air?"

"A rebreather I invented. It's good for about fifteen minutes. Are you okay?" Agent X answered, sitting up and touching Betty's face.

"I'm fine, but you're bleeding! And that madwoman is still out there!" Betty Dale almost yelled, touching his injured arm.

"I'll be fine; I know where she'll be." Agent X stated and stood up. He helped Betty to her feet and added, "She told me and she's not as clever as she thinks."

"Where is she headed?" Betty asked, not remembering what was said earlier.

"Simple enough..." Secret Agent X stated and led her towards the exit.

The Statue of Liberty stood proud and majestic overlooking Manhattan. Agent X was always amazed by this wonderful monument, a powerful symbol of freedom for the whole world. France's gift to the United States was often the first sight immigrants saw upon entering the country. It was also his first sight upon returning from the Great War, a moving tribute to the reason the war was fought. Lady Liberty was the representation of the best of the country and Agent X was always moved when catching sight of the incredible statue.

The fact that Madam Rogue's pretender referred to the statue as "France's Folly" was merely another exampled of the madwoman's arrogance. She was dangerous and, if X had not been involved, may have murdered many more people and stolen untold numbers of precious pieces of art. But in her pride she threw the glove of challenge at Secret Agent X and her plans began to crumble. Sadly, lives were lost before X could confront this fiend.

Walking into the Statue, Agent X began slowly climbing the winding stairs towards the crown. The Madam Rogue pretender was nowhere in sight, so X continued to climb towards the torch Lady Liberty held above her head. Unsurprisingly, the pretender was standing there, her hood restored, hands behind her back.

"Very dramatic." Agent X sneered, trying to enrage the woman and cause her to make a mistake.

"You seek to anger me? Do not bother. These will be your last moments of life." Madam Rogue's pretender replied, her mechanical voice as flat as before. She removed her hands from behind her back, revealing a pair of epee swords. She tossed one to X, who caught it with his uninjured left hand.

"A duel? That's how you view this battle?" X asked, shocked despite himself.

"Yes, let us test to see who is the greater warrior!" Madam Rogue's pretender stated, raising her sword in salute.

X shook his head and raised his sword in reply. And then they were off, their blades flashing like lightning bolts in the darkness. They stepped back and forth, the only sound the clash of metal as the blades sought the blood of their opponent. Round and around the torch they circled, with X on the attack at times, on defense in others. Slowly Madam Rogue's pretender became the attacker more and more, her skill far greater than that of Secret Agent X.

"You should know," Madam Rogue's pretender said in her robotic voice. "I am considered the greatest sword master in all of Europe. I assume you are the same for this country."

"Nope," X replied with a head shake. He was growing tired and knew he was outmatched in this skill. "A man named Wentworth holds that title. I'm just a student."

"Then allow me to school you." Madam Rogue's pretender leaped to the attack. Her blade flashed out, slicing X's cheek and then pricking his shoulder, clearly toying with her opponent. Finally she stomped the ground and with a flourish, swept the sword from Agent X's hands. The blade spiraled over the rim on the torch, falling to the Earth far below.

"You fought well, my enemy. And as a tribute, I shall kill you quickly." The new Madam Rogue's stated and stabbed for X's chest.

But Agent X was not there, he was already moving on an angle just away from the sword. With a roar, his leg slashed out, the shin striking his enemy in the face and shattering the woman's nose. Landing forward, his lead hand crashed down on the her wrist, shattering the bones and causing the sword to clatter to the floor.

"I was only an amateur at sword fighting," Agent X explained as he picked up and tossed the sword off the side of the torch. "I always preferred my hands and feet. You see, swords can be taken away."

"But! But!" The pretender stammered, stumbling backwards.

X tilted his head to the side, pretending to try and understand the woman. "You thought I would duel you in some foolish contest? No, this isn't some penny dreadful despite your dramatics. Now, last chance to fight back!"

The Pretender jumped to her feet, pulling a gun from her waistband. X kicked out again, breaking the Pretender's other wrist and sending the gun spiraling off the side.

Backing away, the Pretender struck a fighting pose, "As you wish, barbarian. But you should know, I am a maestro of the French art of foot fighting, Savate!"

"Oh good," Agent X replied with a nod, "I am too. Let's see what you know."

The duel began again, but with flashing legs instead of steel. They moved back and forth for several minutes. But then Agent X's right fist pistoned out, striking the woman's jaw and sending her spiraling back, crashing into the statue's flame and crumpling to the ground.

"You...cheated..." The Pretender stated, trying to stand but collapsing.

X shook his head, "I now understand you. You're a child. To you, this was a duel against your mother's former student. But it wasn't that, not at all. I'm not some mythical hero for you to defeat or some rival to your mother's legacy. I'm a man who wanted to save the lives of people you planned on killing. I won't kill you. No, that I'll leave in the hands of Lady Liberty's sister, Blind Justice!"

With that, Agent X pulled out another of his gas guns and fired, knocking out the Pretender. He then slung the woman over his shoulder and began the long walk down the stairs.

Postscript:

Madam Rogue's Pretender, as she was known in the newspapers, sat huddled in her cell in the lowest part of the jail known as The Tombs. Her trial would start soon and apparently the police, and their unofficial friend Secret Agent X, produced a case that her lawyer assured her was airtight.

She was about to begin cursing Secret Agent X again when a shadow crossed her face. A figure surrounded by darkness stood before her, unmoving. The shadowy figure did not seem to breathe, it was as if the darkness came to life and formed the shape of a human being.

"Mother?" The Pretender rasped, her mechanical voice not hiding the terror in her tone.

"You sought to take my name? Foolish move, my child. No matter, once I am done with you I shall destroy the one known as Secret Agent X!" Madam Rogue stated, in a light and musical voice. She then moved forward and the Pretender began to scream...

THE END

A LITTLE THANKS....

Gratitude. It's an emotion never really expressed enough, even by writers like myself. I do try and pay some tribute to influences throughout my life as a writer, but it never felt enough. I always wanted to pay tribute to more people over the years, but never found the right occasion. Therefore instead of writing about how I created the story you just read, I'd rather spend some time saying thanks to all the people that helped me become a writer. One caveat; I'm sticking to people I actually know, otherwise the majority of this essay will be about Harlan Ellison, Philip Jose Farmer, Stephen King, Howard Hopkins and other giants who made me want to reach for the stars.

The first person I have to thank is Jean Marc Lofficier. JM (as his friends all call him) brings a lot to the table, writer, editor, publisher, historian... the list is long because he's an impressive man. JM gave me a chance to be a writer, allowing me a chance to be published in *Tales of the Shadowmen* along with such legends as Michael Moorcock and Brian Stableford. The chance he took on me made it possible for me to be a writer.

Next is my long-time pal Win Scott Eckart. Win and I knew each other for about a decade online through some discussion groups on Philip Jose Farmer's great works. It was odd relationship, a good friend you know through email and Facebook only until we met at Pulpfest and if anything we got closer. Why am I thanking him? Because all those times I was rejected and feeling low he was one of the first to pick me up and occasionally kick my butt out of the pity parade. Every writer needs that type of friend.

Third is an easy one, my friend and publisher Ron Fortier. Ron and I also met online through his blog. I was a fan of Ron's comic work, especially the Green Hornet and I wrote him to ask him a question about something. I'm sure it was some silly fanboy nonsense, but he kindly wrote me back and we got to talking on pulp and writing. After a night of probably 20 or so emails, he gave me a shot at writing my favorite pulp hero, Secret Agent X. That's how I got here, pure and simple. Ron's gamble paid off for me big time, I'm a writer thanks to him. Oh and I should add, he's an amazing editor who taught me a great deal over the years.

Thanking Shihan James Amorosi is essential to my life, not doing so would be like forgetting to breathe. Shihan (the Japanese word for a martial arts master) is a mentor in a very real sense, the man who has been there for me in so many ways I could write an essay on him alone. Besides teaching me to believe in myself enough to take a chance to be a writer, he's the person who's made it clear he expects me to try 100% in all things in life. "Don't settle for being mediocre" is one of his mantras for me and I'm such a different person since I started training under him over a decade ago.

Next is another easy one, artist and publisher Rob Davis. Rob is another person I met online but was fortunate enough to meet in real life. Rob is such a decent person, a calm but strong voice of reason whose art always manages to blow me away. The first time I met Rob, he showed me the artistic and business side of publishing, something that matured me as a writer in a very positive way. Also he was the first person in the pulp world I met that shared my love of Secret Agent X, which made me want to write the character even more over the years.

Oddly enough the next person I want to thank is also an artist, Jay Piscopo. Jay is probably the most talented, imaginative person I've ever met in my life. An artist of uncanny skill as well as a writer who's work continually blows me away, Jay is a good friend and supporter since we met. Jay always manages to challenge to try even harder, to try and expand the world of pulp we both love. Every writer needs someone like that in their life, a good friend who wants you to succeed and be your best.

To not thank my mother, Ruth Schildiner, would be just patently ridiculous. My mom and my late dad are the reason I love pulp, monster movies and film noir. They introduced me to that list and indulged my somewhat obsessive love of all my interests, reading countless Godzilla, Frankenstein and Dracula tales I wrote over the years (and kindly not telling how dreadful those attempts were, I was no Stephen King). One of my running jokes over the decades is I'd never be a successful writer because I came from a happy, sane home thanks to having amazing parents.

Last, and by no ways least is my wife Gail Schildiner. Gail is my top supporter, always in my corner and completely unimpressed by my writer based obsessions and bouts of anger. Stephen King often writes how his best supporter is his wife, who also is unimpressed by his "greatness". Having someone who loves you, cares for you and tells you to get over yourself makes life worth living. That's Gail, and I'm lucky to be with her for over 20 years.

There you have it, a little dose of gratitude to people in my world. This is faint praise for all of the above people, but I hope they all realize it's from the heart. Thanks one and all, every book or short story I write is thanks to you all.

FRANK SCHILDINER - has been a pulp fan since a friend gave him a gift of Philip Jose Farmer's *Tarzan Alive*. Since that time he has published articles on Hellboy, the Frankenstein films, Dark Shadows and the television's Lovecraftian links. He is a regular contributor to the fictional series *Tales of the Shadowmen* and has been published in Secret *Agent X* Volumes 3 and 4 and, *Black Bat Mystery* by Airship27, *The New Adventures of Thunder Jim Wade* and *The New Adventures of Richard Knight* by Pro Se Production and *The Avenger: The Justice Files* by Moonstone. Frank works as a martial arts instructor at Amorosi's Mixed Martial Arts. He resides in New Jersey with his wife Gail who is his top supporter.

OCCULT DETECTIVES

They battle demons and monsters, hunt ghosts and defend us against the things that go bump in the night. They are Occult Detectives and they've been a staple of pulp fiction since the beginning of those glorious, garish magazines. Now Airship 27 Productions is thrilled to bring you a quartet of tales starring some of the most unique Occult Detectives ever created; three newly minted heroes and one classic master of mysticism.

From the days of the Wild West, Joel Jenkins offers up his Indian Shaman hero, Lone Crow. Then we have Josh Reynold's colorful Charles St. Cyprian, the Queen's own Royal Occultist, followed by Jim Beard's Sgt. Janus, the Spirit Breaker. And we culminate with a little known pulp classic figure, Ravenwood: the Stepson of Mystery as chronicled by Ron Fortier.

Get ready to take on possessed gunfighters, eerie mesmerizing spirits, a bewitching temptress and a legion of the undead as these four brand new tales usher you into thrilling adventures beyond the realm of the ordinary; your guides....the Occult Detectives.

PULP FICTION FOR A NEW GENERATION!
FOR AVAILABILITY INFORMATION: AIRSHIP27HANGAR.COM

HORROR HAS A NEW FACE

From the pages of the classic pulps comes the most frightening avenger of them all, the Purple Scar!

The handsome, debonair Dr. Miles Murdoch was a world famous plastic surgeon. His life was the stuff of dreams until it all turned into a heart-wrenching nightmare. Murdoch's brother, a dedicated police officer, is brutally gunned down while on patrol. Before dumping his body into the river, his murderers pour acid over his face as a final act of contempt. When the body washes ashore days later, Officer Murdoch's face is beyond recognition, a scarred, purple visage unlike any horror ever imagined.

It is the sight of this death grimace that transforms Miles Murdoch into an avenging angel. Vowing to bring justice to those responsible, the skilled surgeon molds a pliable rubber mask from that repulsive, mutilated face; a mask he dons to become the Purple Scar, the scourge of crooks and villains everywhere. He has become the physical embodiment of their worst fears brought to fiendish life.

Airship 27 now presents four brand new adventures of the creepiest pulp hero of them all, *the Purple Scar!*

www.ingramcontent.com/pod-product-compliance
Lightning Source LLC
Chambersburg PA
CBHW071241250626
47163CB00001B/279